THE LUPIN FIELDS

HEATHER REYBURN

For My Mother, Margaret

CHAPTER 1

September 1966

Dawn Simpson hadn't cried since the day her grandmother was buried, six years earlier, and she certainly would not cry now.

Have I made a huge mistake?

She clasped the letter firmly in her fingers. Butterflies swirled inside her as she and John approached the dwelling—a weatherboard cottage perched in the middle of an empty paddock, stark and forlorn. The wire netting surround, its shiny new posts glistening in the afternoon sun, reminded her of the ugly mesh that imprisoned her old school grounds.

The green Chrysler Valiant hit a bump and she clutched the dashboard, turning to meet her husband's grin and her heart skipped a beat. John's blue eyes crinkled at the corners, the creases fanning into pale lines against his handsome, tanned face while a row of tight curls edged his forehead. She smiled fleetingly and returned her gaze to the building. *This can't be it. We must have to travel farther over the farm yet.*

While he negotiated piles of gravel, she recalled the conversation she and her best friend, Ann, had shared a year ago.

"I'm going to marry a farmer." Ann had been quite adamant, ignoring Dawn's eye roll. "Farmers are wealthy because the government provides subsidies, and the money that wool and meat are bringing are at an all-time high. Plus, they can please themselves what hours they work."

Dawn hadn't argued. She had never visited a farm, or taken any interest in country living, so how would she know if Ann was telling the truth? If Dawn married at all, she'd decided it would be to a man who worked in the city and drove a fine car—someone who would take her on holidays to Australia and cruises to far-off lands. And, of course, be a good father to the horde of children she planned to have.

It's me who's married a farmer, and you're the wife of a builder, so we both got that wrong.

The vehicle slowed and came to a stop, facing the dwelling.

The sturdy timber cottage was exactly like dozens of other New Zealand post-war houses. Its tiny front porch and vacant, staring windows bore no resemblance to what she had envisaged. While the relocated dwelling had been moved to its new destination on

Fantail Ridge, she was spending long hours at the salon basin, shampooing customers' hair and dreaming about her new life. In addition to the new home, her wish for a cat and perhaps a dog would finally be realised, especially as she no longer had to contend with her mother's dislike of animals.

As she stared in dismay, she fidgeted with the envelope. Where was the low-set building with a veranda along the front and French doors opening onto it from every room?

Her glance dropped to the letter. It had been delivered to the Fantail Ridge homestead where John's parents, Harry and Alice, had welcomed them with a delicious lunch, a pile of mail, and boxes of wedding presents. Ann's card was on top and the only one Dawn had opened. It wasn't a gushy wedding card covered with bows and glitter; this was plain white and featured a pair of pretty fantails on the front. Inside, the script was all Ann's—short, sweet, and to the point. Dawn could remember every word.

Dear Dawn,

By the time you get this, you will have returned from your honeymoon and be enjoying the beauty and privacy of your very first home. Congratulations!

I can't wait to hear all about it. Please write soon.

Meanwhile, remember my favourite saying: "There are two types of people in this world. Doers and dreamers. I'm the first and you are the second. So live your dream and share it with me so I can dream with you—or at least, try.

Lots of love to you both,
Ann
PS – Do you like the card? I thought it very appropriate considering you're now living on "Fantail Ridge".

Perhaps she was right. John had been enthusiastic about the purchase. "A perfectly well-maintained house," he'd said. "No longer required —new development on Auckland's outskirts. You don't have to worry about a thing."

In the flurry of excitement, an old, stylish house, filled with character, had filled her mind—something similar to the only home she had ever known.

She inhaled deeply as she stared at the disappointing dwelling. Ugh. What was she going to do? But she already knew. She was going to have to consider herself lucky to have a husband and a place to live.

"This is it. Our new home," John said. He took Dawn's hand and rested it on the leather seat between them. Not a shrub, a tree, or any sign of life near the building. She swung her gaze from the house to her husband and her dismay grew.

"Oh." She bit her lip as her mother's voice resonated in her head. "You said the house was nice—not something the government would provide for the homeless."

Silence filled the car for a few moments as she faced John's apologetic smile. He opened the door and got out slowly, quietly. His hand trailed lightly on the bonnet as he made his way to the passenger side, his eyes fastened on hers. Years of arguments and reaction to her mother's sharp tongue had not served her well, and now she wished she had been taught to look for positives instead of always dwelling on the negatives.

John wrenched the door open and held out his hand. Their love was new and fragile, and the last thing she wanted to do was upset him.

"I'm sorry, darling. You and your parents have done your best. I'm just tired," Dawn said.

"And a bit grumpy?" He gave a wry grin as she swung her long legs out of the vehicle. A gust of wind caught her fair curls, blowing them across her face. She raised a hand to her brow, grateful for the few seconds to bury her head against his shoulder and hide her disappointment.

Am I like my mother? Suppressing the moan that threatened to escape, she stepped back and met John's eyes, willing her own to fill again with hope and fervour. Her chest tightened as something warm unfurled within it. She had promised to have and to hold, for better, for worse, for richer, for poorer … She plastered a smile on her face and reached out. *I must not dampen his infectious enthusiasm.* "Are you going to carry me across the threshold?"

"Of course," he rasped.

For a split second, her legs remained glued to the ground, her eyes resting on the solid, tightly closed door of the cottage. She leaned forward as John swept her into his arms, one work-roughened hand around her back and a strong arm under her knees. After kicking open the ornate wrought-iron gate, he carried her up the path and fumbled with the handle, almost dropping her in the process. Dawn tightened her grip around his neck as they fell through the open doorway. They giggled like school children, her outburst seemingly forgiven, and he set her back on her feet.

"Welcome to your home on Fantail Ridge," John said.

She took a deep breath, tentatively looking around as the last frayed threads of excitement faded to apprehension. Chewing the inside of her cheek, she folded her arms over her chest and rubbed her shoulders.

"It's very cold," she said softly.

"It won't be for long. We'll light the fire, and once we've unpacked, it'll be perfect. The windows let plenty of sun in, and it's small enough to keep cosy and warm." John wrapped her in a tender hug and she leaned against him for a moment, her face pressing against the pulse in his neck. *Life. Live. Love*, his beating heart reminded her.

"That's true." She raised her eyebrows. His excitement was contagious, and she wrestled with her feelings, determined to keep her bluntness under control. It had severely narrowed her field of friends in the past.

"Plenty big enough for us." John released one arm, flinging it in a sweeping gesture and tangling a lock of her shoulder-length hair in his fingers.

"Ouch!" Her hand flew to her head, and his eyes widened in horror.

"Oh, I'm so sorry. I'm such a clumsy twit." He squeezed her against him. "Are you alright?"

She nodded briefly and gazed around the room—if you could call it that. It was more of an enclosed porch. A row of coat hooks adorned the inside wall and a brand new wringer washing machine stood in the corner, nestled against the double concrete laundry tub.

"The laundry?" she asked.

Why hadn't they come through the front door? She hadn't even noticed a front entrance. Consumed with disappointment, she had barely registered the garage and gate that led them to where they now stood.

"Yes, sort of. I suppose it's the room for everything that doesn't have its own space. We'll have the wood box in here over winter, and this cupboard is where the hot water cylinder is." John opened a door to reveal a slim, silver tank surrounded by shelves, and she allowed herself to relax a smidgeon as the warmth emanating from the cupboard wafted around her.

"Plenty of space because it doubles as a linen cupboard." He closed the door again and flung open the one next to it, a little less enthusiastically this time. "Bathroom and toilet."

She nodded, a shadow of a smile hovering around her lips. John grasped her hand again and towed her into the small hallway.

Peering into each room as they passed, she tried hard to be optimistic. In the first, a fixed bench against the inside wall provided seating while a small wooden table squeezed between it and the kitchen sink. *Not a good start.* Her heart sank even further. It certainly wasn't the large country kitchen where she dreamed they would spend most of their indoor time, with newspapers and magazines spread over the table and room for her to bake while their children scattered toys across the floor.

"New electric stove, just for you," John said, enthused, as he pointed to the appliance at the end of the Formica bench, and then to the window. "A great view, don't you think? Plenty of warning if visitors are coming." He laughed and grasped Dawn's hand again, gently guiding her out of the room and back into the hallway.

She glanced into the two small rooms on either side of the hall. *Bedrooms?* Four strides led them to the end of the passage, opening into a cosy lounge with a fireplace on the southern wall. Facing east, a large window provided a multi-layered view across the paddock to the Kaipara Harbour. Beyond its sparkling waters, the mainland spread across the horizon, shadowy and distant.

Dawn fixed her gaze on the panorama. All her life she had been a city girl, and now, in spite of the beauty in front of her, a shiver ran down her spine. Exposed and helpless, she reached out and clutched the heavy maroon curtains hanging on either side of the window, the urge to close them so strong she had to steel herself. Taking a slow, deep breath, she studied the fabric as she forced her hands to drop to her sides. *Shabby, but serviceable. They'll do until I can find something better.*

John touched her arm and turned her to face a small, enclosed front porch leading off the lounge. "I should have brought you through here. You would have got a better first impression. Sorry, love."

She shot him a brief grin and followed his gaze through the second doorway into what was clearly the main bedroom.

"Ours. Doesn't the furniture we chose look good? It was only delivered the day before our wedding, so I left Mum to get it ready and make it welcoming for you," he said.

Dawn nodded, annoyance preventing her smile from reaching her eyes. Studying the plain white cotton bedspread and green eiderdown lying diagonally across the bed, the words stuck in her throat. One thing was certain—no matter how much she and John loved each other, she would be redecorating the house to suit her own tastes. How she would achieve this without offending her mother-in-law would be something she'd worry about later.

CHAPTER 2

"What do you think of your new home?" Alice asked as she poured Dawn a cup of tea.

"It—it's fine." Dawn shrugged.

A wave of concern swept over her mother-in-law's face and Dawn squirmed. She glanced toward the window seat on the other side of the room, relieved to see John and Harry deep in conversation and apparently unaware of her response.

"You'll be wanting to settle in and make it your own but if you need help with anything, please ask. I suppose your mother will be keen to make new curtains and all sorts of bits and pieces for you, being the efficient seamstress she is," Alice continued, her voice quiet.

Dawn gave her a half-hearted grin and attempted to swallow her resentment. A dressmaker her mother may have been, but as for sewing soft furnishings for her daughter—well, the likelihood of that was zero. She could hear her mother's voice nagging in the recesses of her memory. *"Unpick it and start again. I won't be around to help you when you grow up so you'd better learn to do things now."*

Returning her attention to Alice, a fleeting stab of guilt pricked her. Her mother-in-law's kind, round face with its peaches and cream complexion looked pinched, anxious, accentuating a nose that was a little too large to fit with her petite bone structure. Alice had not only prepared their bedroom, but she also filled the fridge and pantry with a variety of groceries, fresh vegetables, and eggs, while Harry had apparently spent days building the fence around their house. During their period of generosity and hard work, Dawn and John had been languishing in the Bay of Islands, walking, eating, and revelling in each other's company.

These people are so undeniably kind.

"Um ... I don't know what to call you." Dawn touched her cheeks as they flushed pink. Unsure how to address John's parents on the few occasions they had met, so far she had managed to avoid having to.

"Alice and Harry? The grandchildren call us Granny and Grandad but our daughters-in-law call us by our names. At least that way, we know who you are talking to." Alice smiled and laid a hand on Dawn's shoulder. The soft fragrance of talcum powder mixed with a hint of cloves from the apple pie they'd recently demolished wafted over her, and Dawn's face flamed brighter.

Dawn loved her mum, but in spite of being her only child, Lillian had never been the motherly figure that she had longed for. She missed her gran more than ever.

"You must be tired," Alice said. "John, I think it's time to take your lovely wife home."

Dawn looked up as John pushed his chair back. "Gladly."

"I'll just use … umm." Dawn pointed to the hallway and hurried from the room, the thought of her grandmother bringing a lump to her throat.

As she returned from the bathroom, Dawn trod quietly and paused outside the open door to gain her composure—in time to catch Alice's softly spoken question.

"Do you think she will be happy here?"

"Yes, of course, Mum. It may take a while. Remember, she's only ever lived in a big city—and since her grandmother died, her main influence has been her difficult and crabby mother. Not the best situation to have been raised in. Don't worry. She'll soon realise we're very different—and I've got plenty of patience."

Dawn stepped more heavily and gave a cough as she entered. Love surged within her for her husband, and she moved to his side.

He lay his arm over her shoulders, grinned at his father, and kissed his mother on the top of her head. "Thanks for the lovely meal, Mum."

Alice smiled and turned to face Dawn. "If it's alright

with you, dear, I'll pop up about mid-morning with some fresh baking and help you unpack some of those wedding presents."

Dawn nodded mutely. In spite of wanting to have control over everything in her new house, how could she refuse this sweet lady's offer?

TAPPING HIS FINGERS ON THE STEERING WHEEL, JOHN hummed as they drove back up the hill and across the paddock to their home, the glow of headlights the only light in a world of darkness.

"This time, we'll go in the front door so you can see your house from a different perspective—just like a visitor will when you get to know a few people around here and have them call in for a cuppa." John squeezed her hand, and Dawn smiled gratefully.

Stepping carefully over the damp grass, she followed him along the side of the house and up the steps into the dark, enclosed porch. She rubbed the tops of her arms while he fumbled with the front door, relieved when it burst open and the warmth from the fire they'd lit earlier enveloped them. Flames pirouetted behind the mesh screen, greeting them like tiny fairy dancers, and her spirits lifted a notch. Perhaps once they had slept and she could unpack properly, the house would grow on her and feel more like a home? She certainly hoped so.

John pulled the two armchairs closer to the fire. "Why don't you get ready for bed while I make us a cup of cocoa? We can sit here and get you warmed through while we drink it."

Dawn nodded and a soft smile spread over her face as she watched her husband stride towards the kitchen with a lightness in his step.

At ten years her senior, he had been an attentive, generous, and caring suitor. His visits to her Epsom home had become more frequent as the months had progressed. Regular walks to the park and local cafe were the highlight of his visits, leaving her mother at home to prepare tea for them all before he headed back to the farm. Delight and relief had overwhelmed her when he'd produced her pretty engagement ring and asked her to marry him. She grinned inwardly as she remembered listening at the door while he solemnly and fervently asked her mother for permission to take her as his bride. At this moment, with him prancing about like a teenager, it was hard to compare that serious man with the one she called her husband. Suddenly, she felt older than her twenty years.

Turning to the window, she stared into inky blackness, clouds preventing even tiny pinpricks of stars from lighting the sky. There were no comforting streetlights or warm glow from neighbour's house windows. Cold ripples of isolation crept over her. There was only silence—not a car, no laughter or conversation from pedestrians walking by, not even the bark of a dog. A shudder consumed her and she snatched at the curtains, jerking them across the icy, dark glass, then hurried to the bedroom.

After quickly stripping off her slacks and blouse, she slipped a silk nightgown over her head, wrapped herself in her comfy chenille dressing gown, and curled up on the lounge, allowing her mind to drift.

It was hard to believe that this time last year, she'd had no idea of John's existence. Her mood lifted as memories flooded back. It had started to rain and she was late for the bus. Stepping out of the hairdressing salon, her home away from home for the past four years, the heel of her new patent leather shoe had caught on the door sill and she'd pitched forward, landing on her hands and knees right in front of a pair of scuffed and slightly muddied brogues, and dark trousered legs. Her handbag had hit the pavement and burst open, spilling its contents across the path.

As quick as lightning, the legs had knelt in front of her, an arm grasping hers and a large, weathered hand swooping up her lipstick, coin purse, and, horror of horrors, the zipped packet containing her sanitary items.

Dismayed, she had looked up, straight into a pair of striking blue eyes. Light brown hair, dampened by raindrops, topped the worried face.

"Are you alright?" The man asked and she struggled to her feet with the aid of his firm grip on her elbow.

Pulling her tight skirt towards her knees, she stuttered, trembling with embarrassment and shock.

"I—I'm fine thanks. I tripped on the step." Her knee stung and she glanced down to see a trickle of blood running down her shin and a large ladder forming in her stocking.

"Let me help you." His voice was soft, and he shoved the items back into her handbag, closed the clasp, and led her towards the salon door and out of the rain. "Would you like to go back inside?"

"I'll miss my bus." She bit her lip and glanced around swiftly, apprehensive about accepting the man's help and hoping no one else had witnessed her fall.

"I think you should sit down for a few minutes. My car is parked only a few yards away and I can take you home."

She stared at him in a quandary for a few seconds before the salon door was pulled open and the senior hairdresser appeared in the doorway.

"Dawn! Are you alright?"

Nodding, she allowed herself to be pulled inside again, closely followed by her rescuer.

"Hello. I'm Linda, Dawn's colleague. And you are?"

Dawn fixed her gaze on the young man, noting his friendly smile, the row of straight white teeth, and the way his eyes crinkled at the corners. His open-necked shirt and casual tweed jacket, combined with the muddied shoes, suggested he was an unlikely banker. He offered his hand to Linda and she took it briefly, smiling at him in her usual gracious but superior manner.

"My name's John Simpson. I'd just left the dentist down the road and was hurrying to my car when I saw this poor girl trip and fall." He turned to Dawn, meeting her at eye level. "And you are Dawn." Smiling widely, he held his hand out and squeezed hers gently. "Are you sure you're alright?"

"Yes, thank you. I'll be fine."

"You must let me drive you home. It's pouring out there now, and you're in no fit state to walk—or wait until the next bus comes along."

After receiving an approving nod from Linda, Dawn allowed John to drive her the three miles to the roomy villa she had grown up in—one of many in the leafy, elegant street in Epsom. Stiff and anxious in the passenger seat, she bit her lip and slid her gaze towards him.

"Where do you live?" she asked.

"South Head. Do you know where that is?"

She shook her head as the heat rose in her cheeks.

"About an hour's drive north of Auckland. We live on a farm two thirds of the way up the peninsula."

"We?" She stared at him, waiting for more.

"My parents and me. I was a baby when we moved there and I've never lived anywhere else. One day, I hope to marry and have a warm and loving home of my own there—like the one my parents provided for my brothers and me."

"And is there a nice country girl in the district for you to marry?"

He grinned at her and she relaxed a little. "Probably. But I'm waiting for someone special. Sounds a bit soppy, doesn't it? But I can't see any point marrying the wrong person."

She raised her eyebrows and took a deep breath as they turned into her street. *How do you know if they're right or wrong?*

Her heart sank at the sight of her mother hovering on the top step, an umbrella in her hand. "Bother!"

"Is something wrong?" John shot her a glance.

"My mother can be … um, a bit difficult at times."

"I'm a big boy. Don't worry."

As John stopped the car, Lillian stared disapprovingly at Dawn through the rain-washed windscreen. Stepping out of the car before her mother had time to speak, Dawn jumped in. "I had a fall, Mum. And this kind gentleman helped me and has driven me home. Perhaps we could offer him a cup of tea?"

Met with John's smiling face, Lillian had frozen, as though contemplating whether to whack him with the umbrella or invite him in.

"Good afternoon." She gave a slight nod, turned, and marched back to the porch without waiting for a response, her brolly held stiffly aloft. Bedraggled and burning with embarrassment, Dawn trailed behind her mother while John brought up the rear.

It had not been the ideal introduction, but Dawn

had accepted long ago that where her mother was concerned, no introduction of a person of the opposite gender would ever be ideal. Before the first cup of tea had been drained, her mother's barrage of questions had Dawn expecting John to leap to his feet and bolt—which would be a shame, as she was starting to like this kind man with the beautiful ocean eyes. He was so attentive—sweet, even–and seemed almost funny at times.

"Where do you live? What do you do? How long has your family been living there? Are they involved in the community?" The inquisition continued and Dawn cringed, surprised at John's patient responses. Elaborating on what he had already told Dawn, he added compliments about Lillian's lovely home and her daughter's good manners and apologised for not telephoning to advise her he was bringing Dawn home. Dawn sat in stunned silence as her mother's demeanour morphed from stern-faced disapproval to something resembling a smile, like a butterfly emerging from its chrysalis. It appeared the process of drinking tea and nibbling on dry biscuits was all it took for Lillian to actually approve of this man—a total stranger until an hour ago. By the time they said their goodbyes, she appeared well and truly smitten.

Dawn stared at her as she closed the door and turned around.

"Don't look at me like that. You could do a lot worse," Lillian said.

Curled under the eiderdown later that night, the evening's events had replayed again and again in Dawn's head. No matter how hard she tried, she could not rid herself of the shock. John's kind, friendly, and handsome face had, in the space of a little over an hour, shown a completely different side to her cold, hard mother—one Dawn had never had the privilege of knowing.

———

AND NOW, HERE SHE WAS, MARRIED TO THAT KIND stranger—yet still plagued with sadness. Had she got things horribly wrong? It was much later that night, while John breathed noisily beside her, that Dawn turned on the lamp and opened the brand-new packet of writing paper Ann had given her as a 'going away' gift.

Dear Ann,

Thank you for your lovely card. It's the only one I've read so far, and you were right. You are the doer and I'm the dreamer. Only this time, my dreams got it wrong—very wrong.

I wish you were here, but you're not, so this letter will have to do. The house is awful! It's tiny, cold, and boring. John lit the fire, which helped, but it's still horrible. Remember that block of public houses we used to walk past on the way to school—designed for shelter but not style? Well, it's one of those. A wooden box with no veranda, no

French doors, no garden, and it's stuck in the middle of a paddock miles from anyone or anywhere.

John's parents have the homestead—obviously. It's much bigger and has beautiful plasterwork on the ceilings, a big kitchen, and is surrounded by a stunning garden. I didn't expect the same, but I thought they would provide us with something I could call a home and not just 'a house'. After all, John is the only son who stayed on the farm, so he deserves it—don't you think?

Am I being unreasonable? I am too shocked to cry (not that I would anyway). I can only hope that tomorrow, things will look a bit brighter. Perhaps I am overtired.

Meanwhile, thank you for being my best (and only) friend—except John, of course (and I don't want to say any more to him about my disappointment. He knows!). He is so happy and enthusiastic, and I do love him very much.

How is your pregnancy going? Are you feeling well – "blooming" as the saying goes?

I hope they hurry up and put a phone on in the house so I can ring you and talk.

Lots of love,

Dawn

She folded the paper and slid it into an envelope before turning off the light and pulling up the eiderdown. It seemed like hours later, the silence of the night broken only by the repetitive call of a Morepork, before she finally succumbed to sleep.

CHAPTER 3

"Good morning!"

Dawn leapt to her feet and turned the volume down before shooting her mother-in-law a half smile.

"I did knock but you mustn't have heard me." Alice inclined her head toward the music pouring from the portable record player in the corner. Her arms were laden with a box with a cake tin perched precariously on top.

"Sorry about that. I found my records so thought the music would keep me company while I unpack."

"Of course, dear. That's a good idea. It's just a little hard to talk over."

Dawn turned the knob another quarter turn and "Calendar Girl" faded into the background.

"I've brought you a cake and some meat. Harry dressed a mutton for us yesterday so there's plenty to fill both our fridges and freezers now. Shall I put them in the kitchen?"

"Dressed a mutton?" Dawn stared at Alice in amazement. Surely mutton didn't have to be dressed.

Alice chuckled. "Sorry, love. I suppose you're not used to some of our country expressions. It means a mutton, that is, a sheep that's been killed and skinned, has been cut into roasts and chops and so on … so it's ready to cook."

Frowning, Alice pushed the thought to the back of her mind. Buying a nicely wrapped package of meat from their local butcher had been much more civilised.

She reached out to take the box from Alice, noting her neat skirt and blouse and a perfectly matching string of beads around her neck.

"I'll take it. Are you on your way to a meeting or something?" It hadn't taken long for her to realise that both Harry and Alice were well respected and deeply involved in the community.

"No, not at all." Alice lifted her gaze to meet Dawn's. Her face lit up and her grey eyes sparkled at Dawn. "If I'm not helping out on the farm, I like to wear something a bit nicer than trousers and old shirts. You never know who might pop in to visit."

Dawn hurried to the kitchen, plonked the box on the table, and took stock of her own attire. Her red slacks were dusty and her sleeveless top, with multi-coloured swirls that had once brightened her fair hair, was now faded. The day was not hot and Dawn had the lounge fire going while, between emptying each box, she had enjoyed twisting and jiving to the music. *This 'popping in' business might take a bit of getting used to.*

She reached for the cardigan slung over the back of the chair, pushed her arms into it, and returned to the lounge. "Shall I make us a cup of tea?"

"Thank you, dear. That would be lovely." Alice swept her gaze around the room. "You've made good progress."

"Hmm. I suppose so. The china cabinet is nearly full." Dawn waved towards the pile of wrapping paper and boxes in the corner of the room. "I hadn't realised how many wedding presents we received. So many glasses and crystal bowls. I certainly won't be short of casserole dishes either. It's going to take a while to get around to inviting all the generous gift givers to see me using them." She raised her eyebrows and picked up a pile of crockery before making her way back to the kitchen.

"You put them away and I'll make the tea," Alice said. "Where is your list of who gave which present?"

Dawn stared blankly. "I haven't made one. What do I need it for?"

"For your thank you cards. You know … to write and thank each person for their gifts."

"Oh. I never thought about that."

"Don't worry. We'll do it after our cup of tea. I'll be able to remember some of them anyway." She grinned. "Quite a few guests asked me for gift suggestions so I've got a pretty good idea of who was giving what."

While Dawn stacked the dessert bowls behind the glass doors of the kitchen cupboard, Alice set out two pretty cups, saucers, and plates, and placed them on the table. She filled the milk jug, then arranged the cake and biscuits on a small oval plate. Dawn filled the teapot before plonking herself on the seat beside the window while Alice settled into the chair opposite.

"John was right. The view from here is very pretty," Dawn said. The early spring day was clear and bright, and jonquils, daffodils, poppies, and a flower Dawn didn't recognise burst from a pot near the fence. Alice followed her gaze while Dawn poured the tea.

"I wondered where John put that pot. I planted them in April so you would have something nice to look until you get a garden growing," Alice said.

"Thank you. What is the name of the lemon and blue flowers in the middle?"

Alice squinted. "Oh, you mean the lupins."

Dawn looked at her blankly. "I suppose so. I know the others are daffodils and jonquils—and the pink ones are poppies."

"To me, lupins are one of the most amazing flowers to grow. They are actually a legume, you know—in the same family as peas and beans."

Dawn didn't know that, but leaned forward, accepting Alice had more to say.

"They're beneficial for providing nitrogen and

stabilising soil. I believe another variety of them are grown as a food crop in places like the Andes where their seeds, or beans, are used as food for both animals and humans—not that I've tried them, mind."

Dawn turned to stare at the flowers, deciding to take a closer look after Alice left.

"I suppose you are dying to get out and start a garden now."

Dawn blinked hard as she digested Alice's comment. "No." She stopped, immediately regretting her quick rebuff. "I—I mean, I hadn't thought about it. Actually, I don't have a clue how to start one. At our Epsom home, Mr Freeman came once a week to tend the gardens and mow the lawn."

In her narrow world, gardening had seemed more of an old person's hobby. She only knew the names of some flowers because, during the long and boring school holidays, she'd pestered him, just as she'd pestered Mrs Bailey when she arrived on the bus every Friday to 'do' for them. While chatting to the woman as she vacuumed and mopped the floors, dusted the furniture, and scrubbed the bathroom, it had never occurred to Dawn that one day she might have to do the same. The only thing she had learned, largely due to necessity, was how to cook a tasty meal for her mother and her, thanks to her grandmother's guidance. When she was alive, Dawn had followed her back and forth across the roomy kitchen, stirring bowls of delicious cake ingredients together so she could lick the spoon and scrape the bowl afterwards. She'd helped peel and chop ingredients for the evening meal and allowed her grandmother to guide her hand while she cut leaves and fashioned roses out of the pastry scraps. At no time in Dawn's life had she witnessed her mother attempting any housework and any cooking she attempted was purely to keep them alive—that was, until Dawn met John.

Aware of Alice's gaze resting on her, Dawn shrugged and replied, "I don't know anything about gardening. Or housework really. Mr Freeman always took care of our garden."

"Oh well, you'll soon learn," Alice said and patted her hand as it rested on the table. "Didn't you help your mother?"

Dawn shook her head, bristling under her mother-in-law's gaze. "Not really. I … we were lucky. There always seemed to be money available, and we had paid help for the inside work as well as outside."

Silence filled the room before Alice spoke again, her tone soft and kind. "I'm sorry your father couldn't walk you up the aisle. You must miss him."

Surprise at Alice's comment rendered Dawn speechless for a few moments while she searched the recesses of her memory. Apart from the photo that sat next to her mother's bed, she couldn't recollect anything about him. Not the colour of his hair or his eyes. Not even the sound of his voice. The only thing that occasionally triggered a familiarity was the smell of pipe tobacco that sometimes drifted around the bus on her way to work.

"I was two and don't remember him at all. I was told he died of pneumonia, and I didn't miss him because we lived with Gran. She filled the gap that he may have had, until she died when I was fourteen."

"Oh." Dawn met Alice's eyes, but Alice dropped her gaze, and Dawn recognised compassion and something else flashing across her mother-in-law's face. Pity? She didn't need sympathy—nor was she going to tell Alice that it was her grandmother who'd lavished Dawn with love and guidance. She had no recollection of either from her parents. It was following her Gran's death that Dawn understood what loneliness really was, and in spite of teenage hopes, the rift between Dawn and her mother had grown ever wider.

"Well. I thought I would invite a few of the local ladies for morning tea next week so you can get to know them. How does that sound?"

Dawn took a deep breath and drew strength from Alice's intended kindness. Moving to the farm might not have been quite what she'd expected, but she was a grown woman. She would certainly not admit her failings. "Fine. Thank you."

———

"Come on. You've been inside for days. It's time I gave you a tour of the farm—and a driving lesson."

John grinned and hugged her before pushing her gently in front of him towards the back porch.

With trembling fingers, she struggled to tie the laces on her sneakers. She buttoned her jacket while butterflies circled wildly inside her stomach.

A tour of the farm was acceptable, and even potentially enjoyable—but a driving lesson was another thing entirely. She steeled herself, urging her heart to slow while her husband opened the truck door and held her arm as she hoisted herself into the passenger side of the cab. Trying hard to be reasonable, she acknowledged there were no buses or trains out here. It seemed there wasn't much alternative but to tame her terror and get behind a steering wheel.

"You're not going to make me learn how to drive this thing, are you?" Her eyes widened as she faced him.

"Not yet. I'll give you a lesson in the car when we get back so you get the feel of operating the pedals and steering in the open paddock. We'll worry about the rest later." He chuckled and patted her knee as she gulped back her dread.

While the vehicle bounced across paddocks and accelerated up steep tracks with its engine roaring, Dawn gripped the dashboard, her knuckles pearly white. By the time she had opened and closed four gates, the knot in her stomach had begun to unravel and, as she leaned on the last post while John manoeuvred the truck through the space, she allowed her gaze to roam the property, pleasantly surprised at the lush, peaceful scene.

On her visit prior to their wedding, John had encouraged her to accompany him and Harry on a routine hay-feeding excursion. She had remained in the relative security of the truck cabin—too afraid to stick her head out of the window in case one of the animals felt like having a chat to her. Now, she breathed in the warm spring air, her eyes scanning the vista as a splash of peace crept over her. Dotted with the occasional house, woolshed, and the neighbours' dairy, the land fell away toward the sparkling harbour, and Dawn allowed the last of her anxiety to dissipate. A pair of colourful ducks flew past, their webbed feet thrust forward. She watched, mesmerised as they skied onto the tiny dam nestled between two folds of land, then tucked their wings neatly against their bodies.

Smiling, Dawn hauled herself back into the truck. "Did you see them?"

John nodded. "Yes, they're Paradise Ducks, endemic to New Zealand, and they're actually a shelduck.

"What's a shelduck?"

"The genus of duck that includes the Paradise." He shot her a grin. "They mate for life and usually nest in the same place each year—just like us, eh?"

She raised her eyebrows and allowed the corners of her mouth to lift slightly. "So the Paradise is something special—not just a duck-duck."

They both laughed and John squeezed her hand.

"I don't think I've seen any before?" Dawn said. *It seems I've got lots to learn.*

"I suppose there are not many who would choose to nest in the city. Much too noisy for them." He grinned and thrust the gear stick forward before proceeding to drive on. By the time they reached the far corner of the paddock, Dawn had relaxed into the rhythmic motion of the vehicle, allowing her body to sway gently against the worn leather seat. They crept toward a ridge and John swung the truck in a circle, coming to a halt as they faced south before switching off the engine.

"Hop out and come for a walk with me," he said.

Dawn sat forward and opened the door before sliding carefully to the ground and dusting off her slacks.

John took her hand and pointed to the white-painted house in the far distance. "That's home."

"Don't you mean your parents' home?" she snapped, turning toward the way they had come. "Isn't that way where ours is?"

"Yes, you're right." If her sharp tone offended him, he ignored it. "It's Mum and Dad's home. Our cottage is hidden behind that belt of trees."

She followed his gaze to the row of macrocarpas that sat thick and tall on the rise between their cottage and where they now stood.

"We're at the farthest corner of the farm, and from here, we can see all we own—at least, all we used to own." A smile formed slowly on his lips and Dawn frowned.

"What do you mean?" *What's going on?*

He placed a hand on each of her shoulders and turned her to face the gate in the top corner of the paddock. "See that track on the other side of the gate?"

"Yes. I may not be Einstein, but I'm not blind."

He chuckled. "If we were to continue along that ridge for a mile or two, we'd come to a road that branches in two directions. One way leads out to join the main road to the Heads, but if we turn left and follow the less used track, we'd meet the entrance gate to our new purchase."

Dawn swung to face him, squinting against the sun. "New purchase?"

John drew a deep breath and pulled her down onto the grass. "I'll explain."

With the warmth on their backs, Dawn leaned against him as he talked.

"Prices for both wool and meat have been pretty high for years but now that Britain is a member of the European Economic Community, our butter, cheese, and lamb exports to the 'Mother Country'—as Dad calls it—have fallen dramatically. Mum and Dad thought it might be a good time for us to expand our farming business and get into more cattle production, especially now we're married and we need to provide for two families. So ... we decided to make the most of every opportunity that comes our way."

Dawn digested this information for a few moments. Politics and trade agreements between countries meant nothing to her, and the realisation of how little she knew or understood about business came as a shock. "And?"

"And that opportunity is the subdivision of government land that runs from here out to the Tasman Sea. Quite a few of the blocks closest to the main road have been offered to returned soldiers, but we've been waiting for the rest to be announced for sales. Now it's been split into four farms of about six hundred and fifty acres each. Perfect for a run-off."

Dawn frowned. "A run-off?"

"A block of land that has good feed and water, although it's often a bit rough. It's the sort of property we can run cattle on when the stock don't need daily attention. In our case, it means we can increase our cattle numbers."

"So ... is Fantail Ridge a lucrative farm? I mean, are we poor or wealthy?" Dawn hesitated.

John rubbed his jaw. "We're neither, really, although we've done okay. As I said, our generation has seen good times, and now that we're here to look after the place, Mum and Dad are talking of going on an overseas trip. That certainly couldn't happen a generation ago."

So, was Ann right or wrong?

"Of course that doesn't mean there's any less work for us. In fact, there's more as we continue to build it up and repay the loan for both our house and the new property."

Dawn's hopes fell to her boots. "Oh."

"Oh?"

She shrugged. "I was thinking we could employ someone to help me around the house and start a garden."

He shook his head and snorted. "Not yet, honey bunch. We've got a lot to do before we take on employees."

"I see," she said. Actually, she didn't see at all. *What does wealthy really mean?*

She scrambled to her feet and strode to the truck. "If you're going to give me that driving lesson today, we'd better go home now."

She fixed her gaze in front of them as they rumbled across the paddocks. Confusion filled her head and she refused to enter into any further conversation.

CHAPTER 4

As soon as she woke on the day of Alice's morning tea, a sense of dread filled Dawn's already waning confidence. She had learned early how to fade into the woodwork. The thought of being the main object of interest increased the pain behind her eyes, and she massaged her temples.

Flicking through her wardrobe, she eventually pulled out a peacock blue dress with a tight waist and wide black belt. The skirt was a little old-fashioned, but at least it covered her knees. *If I am plonked in a circle of old busybodies, I won't have to worry about showing too much leg.* She gathered the loose pieces of hair from either side of her face and clipped them together on top of her head, allowing the balance to hang softly on her shoulders. Low-heeled court shoes completed her outfit and she called out, "I'm ready."

John appeared in the doorway and gave a low wolf

whistle. "Wow. You look fantastic. You'll certainly be sending a few tongues wagging around here."

She grinned as a glow of love warmed her. She stepped closer to him, pressing her face against his. He held her tight and they kissed.

"Whoops. I'll have to redo my lipstick." Reluctantly, she extracted herself from his arms and dashed into the bedroom, swooping the colour over her lips again. Then she picked up her cardigan and followed him out to the car.

———

THE YARD WAS ALREADY FILLED WITH FIVE DIFFERENT vehicles, and she cursed herself for not arriving earlier. Alice had said she didn't need any help. Alice's two best friends, Irene, and Sylvia, would be bringing food to share, and she would be making butterfly cakes and an array of tiny club sandwiches as soon as the chores were completed—certainly in time for the eleven o'clock arrival.

Dawn's face felt stiff as she smiled graciously and lightly touched each of the women's outstretched hands as they were introduced. Seven in all, but no sign of Bev. Dawn had taken an instant liking to her neighbour when she and Alice had visited briefly after Dawn arrived on the farm. Bev's new baby would only be a few weeks old now. *Probably too busy to come today.* Hovering close to Alice, Dawn attempted to answer the barrage of questions and nod politely as her headache intensified.

"Are you enjoying living in the country? Do you ride?

A haughty, twinset-and-pearl-bedecked woman sat it the corner of Alice's formal sitting room, her glare so piercing Dawn was sure it could burn holes in her dress.

"Is someone going to introduce me." the woman's deep-throated command rose above the chatter and Dawn hesitated. *Is she talking to me—or about me?* Before she could react, Irene Bennett stepped in.

"Dawn, this is Mrs Harris. She lives in Auckland now but used to live near Shelley Beach. Mrs Harris was the headmaster's wife in Helensville for many years and I believe she's currently staying with her niece at Mairetahi. Isn't that right, Mrs Harris?" Irene's smile seemed apologetic, and Dawn nodded politely.

Mrs Harris looked Dawn up and down as though she were inspecting a piece of meat. "You're from Auckland, I believe."

Dawn nodded. *Where is this was leading?*

"Where exactly?"

"Epsom. I grew up in Epsom." She cleared her throat, stiffening at the older woman's tone.

"Oh. I expect you would have attended Diocesan School then." It was more of a statement than a question, and Dawn frowned. It was one of the most respected girl's schools in the country, and she had only been able to attend due to her grandparents' legacy—and where that had originated from, she had no idea. "Actually I did. I left in 1961."

"You would have known my daughters. They were boarders of course—and both house captains."

"I was a day girl."

Mrs Harris sniffed—as though something distasteful had been put under her nose. "I see. And what did your father do?"

"My father died when I was very young." Suddenly the woman's questions and hoity-toity attitude grated on Dawn and her patience exploded. "Frankly, I don't see what that has to do with either you or my life here. Please excuse me. I have others to talk to."

She swung away and grabbed a cup of tea from the table. Memories of the small clique of boarders who'd ostracised and terrorised day pupils was the only thing she had been grateful to leave behind. She had otherwise enjoyed her school years and couldn't understand what relevance it had anyway?

As someone touched her arm, she jumped, and tea sloshed over the lip of the cup and onto the tablecloth. Snatching up a serviette, she dabbed at the spreading stain.

"Take no notice of her. She's always been a mean-spirited woman and a gossip. I'm sorry she's here, but she came to visit just as I was leaving home and I felt obliged to bring her."

Dawn looked up into Sylvia's friendly face. She

remembered meeting her at their wedding and she gave her a wan smile. "That's okay. I'm sorry I was rude to her."

Sylvia patted her hand and passed the plate of sand-wiches. "Have one of these. You need something to line your stomach when you deal with people like her."

They shared a chuckle and Dawn did as Sylvia suggested before thanking her and turning back to face the throng of women all vying for her attention.

With her headache persisting, Dawn breathed a sigh of relief when the final car drove away.

"Come on Dawn. I'll take you home now. Perhaps you can swallow some aspirin and have a quiet lie down, dear. I'm sure you'll feel better," Alice said.

To the contrary, an hour later, the headache had dissipated but Dawn felt more wretched than ever.

———

THE FOLLOWING DAY, IGNORING HER POUNDING HEART, Dawn pressed the clutch to the floor and wrestled with the car's gear lever one more time. The vehicle hopped forward, its engine fading then revving loudly as she released her left foot and pushed harder with her right.

"One more lap of the paddock and we'll call it quits," John said.

In silence, Dawn hauled on the wheel, steering the vehicle around the perimeter before depressing the clutch again and changing into a higher gear.

Approaching the house yard, she braked, jerking them both forward. The car stopped suddenly, the engine shuddering into silence.

"Remember to push the clutch in before you stop, otherwise you stall the engine."

"I know that. I forgot," she snapped.

He stared solemnly at her for a second before bursting into laughter.

Relief that the lesson was over flowed through her, and she dropped her hands into her lap and giggled, her annoyance quickly dissipating.

He opened the door, hurried to the driver's side, and bent to kiss her. "You did really well, love. We'll try to do this every day, even if only for half an hour, and by the end of the month you'll be driving like a professional."

"Hmm. I doubt it." She grimaced in spite of a warm glow forming inside her.

———

DAWN CLOSED THE LID OF THE MAILBOX, TUCKING THE pile of letters and newspapers under her arm while she pulled out the bread. Having a fresh loaf delivered six days a week, neatly packaged in its greaseproof wrap, was something that Dawn had not expected. It was a shame the mailman didn't arrive until early afternoon, but it hadn't taken her long to convince John that another hour between eating breakfast and lunch, enabling them to enjoy soft, fresh sandwiches instead of day-old slices that were hard around the edges, was an easy adjustment to make.

In the early weeks of marriage, John hovered around the house with her as much as possible, shifting furniture, hanging pictures, and finishing the house fence and garage. Then, with his return to work alongside his father on the farm, the old habit of joining his parents for lunch and not returning home until dark came as a shock to her. Her disappointment grew into annoyance, and eventually, fury.

She strode up and down the floor of the little house around midday, hoping he would walk in any moment to enjoy the tasty spread of cold meat and salad she had prepared, fuming until she could stand it no longer.

John had barely taken his boots off that evening when her temper overflowed, and she faced him.

"This is your home now. Our home—at least, that's what you keep telling me."

His startled eyes met hers as she spat the words at him. He paused as he leaned over the laundry tub, ready to scrub the dust and dirt from his hands.

"Why don't you come home to have lunch with me more often? Our house is only five minutes from your parents' and I am sick of watching the truck or tractor pull into the yard down there and you not even bothering to tell me you won't be here to eat what I prepare for you." Her voice rose and she finished her rant, breathing heavily.

"I didn't think."

"No, you didn't!" she shrieked. "You don't think. You just do what you've been doing for the last thirty years without a care for me."

John rinsed the suds from his hands as the colour drained from his face. "I'm sorry. Believe me, I would love to come home to you every lunchtime. I'm trying to provide a good income for us, that's all." His voice had remained quiet and low, his tone firmer than she had ever witnessed.

She turned and stomped down the hall to their bedroom, slamming the door behind her.

Lying on the bed, she listened to his footsteps move to the kitchen before the clink of the kettle against the tap and the thump of the fridge door handle triggered a thread of guilt. Replaying her outburst, she admitted he could be right. Nothing here was as she had expected. If only he would recognise how lonely she was. If only he wasn't always so damn cheerful and realised how miserable she was.

It was a relief when, half an hour later, John entered the bedroom, a sheepish grin on his face. He lay beside her and wrapped her in his arms.

"I'm sorry, love. I have been a selfish idiot and I … well I suppose I have continued with my old routine without realising how upsetting it must be for you. I promise I'll be home on the dot of one unless Mum or Dad invite us for lunch. And when they do, I'll collect you so we can all eat together."

Dawn flashed a shaky smile at him. "Thank you. Do you think you could take half a day off work every couple of weeks so we can go to town to shop?"

He chuckled and planted a kiss on her forehead.

"It's a deal."

CHAPTER 5

By late November, Dawn had mastered not only the gears and manoeuvrability of the car but had been venturing to and from the homestead where Alice and Harry were full of praise for her achievements.

The summer evening was warm and mellow as she and John shared the traditional Sunday roast dinner with her parents-in-law.

Dawn pushed her food around her plate while ideas tumbled in her head, destroying her appetite. Giving up on the food, she took a deep breath and squared her shoulders. "I'd like to be more involved."

Three pairs of eyes turned to her and cutlery stilled. John opened his mouth and then shut it again as Harry answered first. "In what way?"

"On the farm?" Alice tilted her head questioningly. "Do you mean you'd like to learn to ride and help with the stock work?"

"Yes. No. Not really. I'm a bit frightened of horses—and the other animals actually. I wondered if perhaps I could start by helping out in other ways." She dropped her gaze to her lap and fiddled with the hem of the tablecloth as her pulse raced and her confidence morphed into desperation. *Don't they get it? I'm bored witless.*

Her agitation grew and she bit her lip as silence stretched for what seemed an age.

"Well, I know it's not farm-related, but we don't have a hairdresser out here and it's often difficult to get away to get our hair cut when it needs it. Perhaps you could offer a small service to some of the locals? You could start with the three of us." Alice patted her snow-white mop and tucked a loose wave behind her ears. "I would like to have mine cut and permed—would you be able to do that for me? We could all pay whatever you suggest so you have a small income of your own. I know it's not easy giving up financial independence, even when the farm account pays the bills."

Gratitude spread through Dawn as she studied her mother-in-law. She did understand. Dawn's self-confidence climbed back to something resembling normal as she shifted her gaze to the men. Harry was almost bald, however, the Friar Tuck fringe that encompassed the base of his skull was ragged and could certainly use a tidy up.

John ruffled his own curly head and grinned at her.

"And I always know when mine's due for a cut when I can't get my hat on properly."

"Right then. I'll bring my scissors with me tomorrow and get you two men sorted out. Alice, I'll write to Linda at the salon and get her to post a few supplies to me. Then I can do your perm, and perhaps the word will spread?"

Alice reached to collect the plates before standing. "Sounds wonderful. One less item for me to have to fit in when I go to town. And don't worry about the word spreading. The bush telegraph is the best source of information you could ever need."

Dawn stood and gathered the used water glasses, grinning as purpose once more flowed through her veins.

———

"Looks good." Dawn placed the tray of sandwiches on the front step and poured three cups of tea. With only two weeks to go before Christmas, John and Harry had almost finished laying the pathway. Its smooth concrete surface ran alongside the new garden bed, leading residents and visitors from the gate to the front door.

"Nothing but the best for my mother-in-law." John grinned and gave her a wink as he ran his hands under the outside tap.

"What day is she arriving?" Harry asked.

"I'm not sure. She said she could only spare a few days so I imagine it could be Christmas Eve." Dawn pursed her lips and crossed her fingers behind her back. Lillian had been noncommittal about joining them for Christmas, and Dawn hadn't dared mention that pulling out at the last minute was a distinct possibility for her mother.

"Oh well. She won't trip over on the path when she does arrive, and by the look of that garden, those flowers will be a picture," Harry picked up a sandwich and peeled a corner of bread back to study the filling. "Yum, cold meat and home-made chutney. My favourite." He took a bite and Dawn smiled, noting the way his eyes sparkled as he chewed. He caught her gaze and swallowed, wiping the crumbs from his bottom lip before speaking. "Don't worry. She can't help but love the place."

Dawn wrapped her hands around the cup and smiled at the flowers, ignoring the lump of uncertainty that was forming in the pit of her stomach. It had been a steep learning curve for her, and she glanced down at her chipped nails. While Alice had enthusiastically moved her kneeling cushion along the bed, digging holes in the rich brown soil, she had encouraged Dawn to follow behind, planting seedlings and firming them down. Stocks stood tall against the house, their buds swelling and a hint of colour emerging. In front of them, the bed was jam-packed with petunias, and alongside the new path, tiny buds crept onto the pansy leaves.

A sense of pride trickled through her belly. By Christmas, she hoped they would be in full bloom, softening the stark cream walls of the house.

She stared past the front yard and across the paddock toward the Kaipara. With no breeze, the water in the harbour was flat, sparkling in the midday sun and lapping at the exposed mud as the tide receded. A flash of movement in the garden caught the edge of her gaze and she turned, narrowing her eyes, and focusing on the newly planted hydrangea shrub near the south side of the house.

"Something just ran under that bush." She put her cup down on the step and bent to have a closer look.

"Probably just a mouse," John said.

"A mouse! Do we have mice?" Dawn leapt back, horrified.

Harry paused, his sandwich inches from his mouth. "Field mice come and go. This is the country, and there'll always be a few around from time to time, especially when the seasons are good and there are lots of grass seed for them."

John laughed and reached out to squeeze Dawn's shoulders. "Don't worry, love. I'll set some traps."

"What you need is a cat," Harry said.

"A cat?" She allowed the exciting possibility to fill her head for a few seconds.

"Seeing as Mum and Dad are going away after New Year's, we might bring the dogs up here to live too, but before we do that, we'll have to build a chicken coop."

Dawn raised her eyebrows, her delight growing at the thought of dogs hanging around the gate. "Chicken coop? I thought we got our eggs from your mother."

"We do, but we need to set up our own too. It's not fair to expect Mum to provide for us as well as them. Anyway, it'll give you something else to do," John finished.

While she packed up the plates and cups, Dawn mulled over the suggestion. The anticipation of introducing a cat, and possibly dogs to the household, was enough to think about. Could she cope with a hoard of feathered friends as well? *Of course I can.*

———

STRIDING TOWARD THE HOUSE WITH THE WIND IN HER face. She didn't hear the farm truck until it was a few yards behind her. She stopped and stood off the track as it rumbled to a halt.

John threw the passenger door open. "Hop in. I've got a surprise for you."

She plonked the bread and mail on the seat between them and hoisted herself onto the leather seat. "A surprise?"

He smiled silently as he drove forward and stopped outside the house gate.

Focused on gathering up the deliveries and clambering out without dropping anything, she started as she lifted her head and almost crashed into John, who had nipped around the truck in record time. She was only a couple of inches shorter than her husband, so meeting him eye to eye was normal, but this time, he stood close and raised his hand to still the movement below his breastbone. Diving a fist inside his shirt, his smile widened as he pulled out a tiny grey and white kitten.

"From Irene Bennett."

Dawn's mouth dropped open. The mail slid to the ground, and she reached across to take the little creature from him. As though understanding it would have to take the lead, the kitten rubbed its head against her hand. She held it out, studying the tiny face before pressing it against her chest and stroking the soft fur. While her smile grew, a rumble from somewhere inside the tiny body vibrated rhythmically against her.

"It's a girl, and she's from a family of good mousers," John said.

Dawn raised her eyes from the kitten. A gentle breeze blew and her gaze shifted from her husband to the tub of poppies waving their heads behind him. "She's gorgeous. I'll call her Poppy."

John grinned again and bent to retrieve the mail and bread before laying his arm across her shoulders. "Poppy it is. Let's have lunch and introduce her to our house."

Joy spread quickly through her as she entered the back room.

My very first pet.

CHAPTER 6

Dawn filtered through the pile of mail with Poppy curled on her lap. A few Christmas cards from John's relations—and one from Ann. After hastily ripping open the envelope, she glanced at the greeting in the card and unfolded the letter.

Dear Dawn,

How are you getting on up there in whoop-whoop land? My heart goes out to you and I understand your disappointment. But unfortunately, sometimes that's reality, and we have to learn how to make the most of things. This can take time. I think of you every time I walk to the shops or catch a bus and wonder how you are coping. Once you have made the cottage your own and can get a few things growing around it, things won't seem so unpleasant.

We are both well and blissfully happy—even if I didn't get to marry a farmer and you did! Graham is very busy working with the building gang. They have two more houses to build before beginning a construction contract for brick units. It seems they are becoming popular with older people who don't want a large yard anymore. The sad part is that many of the units are being built on the grounds where old houses once stood. It seems a shame to bulldoze them for the sake of new houses. I suppose I am just a sentimental fool (not helped by my mixed up hormones).

I am getting rather large now, and the pile of baby clothes I've been knitting and sewing is growing. I miss not being able to go to the picture theatre with you, but Graham and I occasionally see a movie and get fish and chips for tea. I suppose that will all stop when the baby arrives, and he'll be like the other builders and stay late after work for a beer instead.

I saw your mother in the fruit shop the other day. She said she is going to your place for Christmas so I hope that works out well for you both. I admit, I was quite surprised as I can't imagine her on a farm at all!

You haven't told me about the honeymoon yet. I don't need the intimate details but you were very secretive about the destination. Where did you go—and did you have a good time?

Looking forward to hearing from you soon. Have a good Christmas.

Love Ann x

Dawn twisted her mouth and sighed. Ann's pregnancy had been announced only weeks before hers and John's wedding, and Lillian had tut-tutted as she'd let out the side seams of Ann's bridesmaid dress. It was now three months since Dawn and John said their vows and disappointment struck her with increasing intensity as her monthly cycle came around. Ann and Graham's honeymoon had clearly been more productive than her own and a twinge of jealousy crept over Dawn. She pushed away the ache that sat in the pit of her stomach and huffed.

I hate writing letters but I suppose I'd better answer. She tidied up the pile and pushed it to one side before opening the packet of new Christmas cards. Choosing a card with a short commercial message, she began to write in her smallest, neatest writing.

Dear Ann,

Thank you for your card and letter. You know me. I'm the world's worst pen friend—so I'm making this supreme effort just for you!

I'm glad to hear you are well and your pregnancy is progressing as it should. It must be strange for you to walk past the book shop and not have to go into work. I miss the salon and the camaraderie that went with the work, but I'm hoping to find a few customers around the district who need their hair done. No sign of a baby for me, but as we both know, it's early days. Our honeymoon seems so long ago. It was very relaxing and pretty in the Bay of Islands (John's choice, and a good one). We did some fishing and walking and otherwise lay around in the sun (except for two days when it poured rain—and I'm not going to elaborate).

I am slowly getting used to life here, although it is lonely and quiet when John's out on the farm and I'm in the house alone. Actually, quiet is not the right word—but the noises here are not the same as we are used to (if you understand my meaning). Lambing began a few weeks ago and the lambs seem to call for their mothers all day long, or at least their plaintive bleats carry across the paddocks. Alice has a couple on the bottle as their mother's had triplets and couldn't feed them all. They're pretty cute. In the evening they bounce around the paddock playing together, which is really nice to watch. I'm getting used to the calls of the birds and animals but I hate the wind, especially when it howls through the trees on the ridge behind our house and rattles the windows—quite frightening.

When John and I were in town last week, I bought Sandie Shaw's latest record—her new song called "Always Something There to Remind Me". I miss the sing-songs we used to have at your place but at least we have nice memories.

I hope you have a happy Christmas and look forward to hearing from you after the baby is born.

Love Dawn x

Dawn checked what she had written, squinting at the tiny letters, and hoped her friend would be able to read it. Then she slid it into an envelope, addressed it, and withdrew another card from the packet. She scribbled a short note to Linda on the blank inside page, addressed it to the salon, and popped the two envelopes on the windowsill for tomorrow's mail.

How pathetic is that? I have only two Christmas cards to post when Alice sends dozens. Perhaps I'll meet a friend in this community ... someone in a similar position to me?

She crossed her fingers as she stared out of the window, then picked up the kitten and hugged her.

———

PEERING THROUGH THE TORRENT, DAWN SQUINTED AND twirled a lock of her hair as the train pulled into the station. It hadn't been difficult convincing John there was no point in getting out of the car until absolutely necessary.

"I think that's Mum now," Dawn said.

She picked up her brolly, wrestling with the catch as she opened the door. John hurried to her side, his large black umbrella already over his head just as hers opened, almost catching him in the eye.

"Steady on. You're a bit wild with that thing," he shouted over the drumming rain that bounced off every surface and soaked their feet within seconds.

He took her by the arm, and they sloshed through the unexpected downpour to the shelter of the station. Then, squeezing her hand, he leaned into her and spoke softly. "Try not to get upset with her. We both know she can be difficult, but none of us have walked in her shoes—or anyone else's for that matter."

At the exact moment Lillian handed her ticket to the steward and stepped through the gate in front of them, John's words hit Dawn with a jolt. He had been brought up to understand how someone's past could affect their reactions. Thanks to his love and compassion, John had excused her rude and outspoken comments, and she had the grace to feel embarrassed. Gratitude and a deep respect swelled within her. She would try harder to follow his example.

Hugs weren't part of Lillian's agenda. Dawn kissed her mother lightly on the upturned cheek while John reached for her suitcase.

"Welcome to Helensville, Mum," Dawn said.

"Hmm. Not a very comfortable welcome. There wasn't even a sign of rain when I left home."

"Same here. This has come out of the blue so hopefully it will disappear just as quickly." She smiled at her mother and took her arm, holding the umbrella above them both.

Reaching the car ahead of the women, John opened the front passenger door and ushered his mother-in-law inside.

Dawn shook her brolly, closed it, and slithered into the back seat before attempting to dry herself with her handkerchief. The boot door slammed and John landed in the driver's seat beside Lillian, removing his hat with a flourish.

"Phew. That was badly timed." He turned and smiled at Lillian, and Dawn held her breath. *Please be nice, Mum?*

She needn't have worried. Lillian patted tightly permed hair and adjusted her neatly groomed frame in the seat before shooting John one of the most gracious smiles Dawn had ever witnessed. Slumping in the back,

Dawn let her breath out quietly and stared through the window. The rain stopped as suddenly as it had arrived. The sun appeared, and everything around them sparkled.

"Would you look at that," Lillian said. "Mother Nature knew I was visiting for the first time and wants to show me her best."

Dawn blinked hard and retreated to her thoughts while John kept up a running commentary that would have outstripped anything a tourist operator could have shared.

They drove past Harry and Alice's homestead, and Dawn's stomach began to cramp. What would her mother say about their cottage? Would she appreciate the brand-new bed purchased especially for her, with its lilac candlewick bedspread, exactly the shade she liked best? Or would she turn her nose up at the small rooms, the tiny kitchen, and the even tinier bathroom, just as she had. Her cheeks burned at the memory.

Surprisingly, Lillian made no comment, smiling and instead showing interest in the pretty garden now in full bloom, the new curtains hanging in the lounge, and the stunning views from almost every window. John had cut a little pine tree from the thick plantation along the boundary fence, and together, John and Dawn had bought a box of decorations and tinsel on their previous visit to town. Dawn thought it brightened the room immensely and judging by the small smile that played around her mother's perfectly lipsticked mouth, she was hopeful Lillian felt the same way.

Dawn allowed her shoulders to relax and made her way to the kitchen to put the kettle on while John switched on their new television set and invited Lillian to make herself comfortable.

———

CHRISTMAS DAY BEGAN SEDATELY AND DAWN OVERSLEPT, in spite of their early night the previous evening.

"There's a cuppa next to you," John whispered in Dawn's ear and kissed her lightly on the forehead. "I'm nipping over the road to get fresh milk. Be back soon."

Dawn groaned and struggled to a sitting position before reaching for her tea. While she sipped the hot brew, the truck outside whirred into life, then rattled as it bounced across the paddock and faded away.

Having a dairy farm directly opposite their road gate was a bonus and, while she was yet to learn about the industry, she soon realised it was a twice-daily routine that never varied, regardless of what day it was. John had introduced her to their neighbours, Bev and Charlie, soon after moving in and she had warmed to Bev on her second visit with Alice, when she accompanied her to drop off a cake and a small gift after the birth of their third baby.

Appointing himself as the official collector of one billy-full of fresh milk each morning, John's arrangement had suited Dawn as it required an early start—much earlier than she had been prepared for. But her days were long and an early walk each morning might be rather nice, especially as the wretched cockerel had started crowing at some ungodly hour, screeching, and gurgling like a demented banshee. *It will enable me to get to know our neighbours better. I'll start as soon as Mum goes home.*

Guilt flared as she remembered her mother in the next room. *I should have got up to wish her a merry Christmas.* Stepping out of bed, she reached for her dressing gown.

"Merry Christmas, Mum. Would you like a cup of tea?" She waited outside the door for her mother's response.

"Yes please. Merry Christmas."

Dawn re-boiled the kettle and removed a dainty Royal Doulton cup from the china cupboard before opening the packet of Milk Arrowroot biscuits and setting one on the saucer. For as long as she could remember, it had been her morning routine to take a cup of tea and a plain biscuit into her mother. She presumed her grandmother had performed the task before she was old enough to, and she had never minded. When her gran was alive, it gave the two of them a brief window of companionship before her mother rose, and the day's events intruded on their quiet time together. After her death, Dawn used the precious half hour to read while she munched on her boiled egg and slices of toast in the peace and quiet of the kitchen.

"Here you go. Just like old times." Dawn fixed a smile on her face as she placed the cup and saucer on the bedside table. "John's gone to get the milk, and I thought perhaps after his return and we've eaten breakfast, we could go for a little walk so I can show you around."

Lillian's smile faltered. "I'm not really interested in the farm, although the location here is quite pretty. Perhaps we could sit in the garden for a while instead."

Disappointment bit hard as Dawn recalled the number of times she had pleaded with her mother to take her to the park, to feed the ducks, or do anything other than sit in silence in the rambling home while her mother sewed or entertained her bridge group. *Nothing has changed.*

"Of course. We'll do that then. We don't have to go to Alice and Harry's until eleven. John's brothers and their wives and families won't be arriving before late morning, but I did offer to help Alice get lunch organised."

Lillian nodded graciously and drew herself up in the bed. "Very well. I won't get in your way."

Meow.

Dawn beamed as she turned and scooped up Poppy.

"Would you like your breakfast, little one?" She snuggled her face into the soft fur as the kitten purred loudly.

"Don't let that cat in my bedroom, Dawn. You know I'm allergic to animals."

"Sorry, Mum. We're just leaving." Dawn marched out of the room with the kitten in her arms and placed her gently in her basket beside the hot water cupboard.

"Don't worry about her. You and I need to stick together," she whispered.

After returning to the kitchen, she emptied the last of yesterday's milk into a saucer and carried it to the laundry, squatting down to stroke the cat as she lapped. She had only been in the house a few weeks and had well and truly wound her way into Dawn's heart.

If it hadn't been for John's bright and accommodating temperament, for Dawn, the morning would have dragged on forever. After breakfast, she settled her mother in the wooden garden seat with a cushion behind her back, before perching on the bottom step beside John. A breeze blew in from the harbour, bending the flowers in half and a sigh whispered through the pine trees.

"I'm getting a little chilly." Lillian frowned as she drew her cardigan around her.

"Come inside then and we'll open our Christmas presents." John leapt forward and slid his hand under Lillian's elbow, shooting Dawn a wink as he escorted her mother back inside.

Dawn held her breath as Lillian unwrapped the lilac chenille dressing gown, praying that she liked it and wouldn't chastise Dawn. Buying her mother anything had always been difficult. She considered household goods 'boring' and Dawn couldn't afford the only type of gold jewellery her mother would wear. With her first pay, Dawn had bought her mother a pretty silk petticoat, only to be shattered when Lillian scolded her for buying such a personal item for someone other than herself.

"Thank you. It's very nice." Lillian smiled graciously at John first before turning to her daughter. Dawn allowed her breath out in a long, slow release and returned her smile.

Lillian's gifts to each of them filled Dawn with an unexpected warmth. While she unwrapped a pretty apron and fresh white blouse with a 'Peter Pan' collar and tiny pearl buttons, John's gift of a leather belt complete with a pouch to contain his pocketknife struck her as being one of the most thoughtful presents her mother could have chosen.

"Your turn now." John passed Dawn the large colourful parcel from under the Christmas tree and Dawn carefully prised the sticky tape open, revealing a pair of shiny black gumboots. She squealed with delight as she peered inside them, pulling out choco-lates, books, and a dainty gold necklace. Hanging on the fragile chain was a tiny fantail.

Her eyes pricked as she reached over and kissed him.

He rose to his feet and took the necklace from her,

fastening the clasp at the back of her neck. "Now you really are part of Fantail Ridge."

For a few seconds, they stared into each other's eyes, oblivious to Lillian until she reminded them with a sharp cough.

Grinning, John sat down and opened Dawn's gift to him of a new shirt and a book about birds, professing his delight before neatly folded the wrapping paper and tucking it into the sideboard drawer. Then he stood, beaming at both women.

"Come on." He inclined his head toward the hallway. "Back to the kitchen so Dawn can crack on with the food preparation. I'll make us another pot of tea."

While Dawn peeled potatoes, kumara, and pumpkin, and made a large jug of custard, John and her mother sat at the kitchen table. As they gazed through the window, he shared what he knew of the peninsula's history and tales of the characters who lived on it.

"I haven't taken Dawn to visit Paddy yet. He was a wonderful old Irishman who lived with us for as long as I can remember. Died in 1950, and we buried him in the Helensville Cemetery. It's on a hill overlooking the town and harbour, and we thought he would like that. He would have preferred to be buried here, but unfortunately, government acts and laws prevented it."

"Tell Mum about Ed." Dawn had been intrigued by the brief explanation of the Norwegian's story, and she was looking forward to meeting him.

"He's joining us for lunch today, because he lives

alone and has no family, except us." John was matter-of-fact, and a fleeting smile touched Lillian's lips as she inclined her head, as though waiting for more information. Dawn grinned and continued peeling as she listened.

"Ed was washed up on the coastline near here after being shipwrecked, donkeys' years ago. He lived in a shack down by the beach where there used to be a wharf. It's gone now but the boats called in when we first came to South Head to live and our supplies and mail were dropped off and collected from there. Anyway, he became a New Zealander, was sent to war as a naval engineer, and when he returned, he won a little farm farther out in the post-war balloting system. His house is similar to this, and he's set up a dairy and piggery. The cream is collected daily for the Kaipara Dairy Factory, and the milk goes to feed the pigs."

"By farther out, do you mean here on this peninsula?" Lillian had leaned forward and rested her hands on the table as she appeared to listen intently.

John nodded and Lillian's smile widened.

"I'm looking forward to meeting him."

Dawn returned her attention to the sink and pursed her lips. Her mother had always taken an interest in people from far-flung nations. Far more than she did her own daughter.

CHAPTER 7

On their arrival, John helped his father insert the two extra panels in the centre of the table and carry extra chairs from the shed while Dawn and Alice assembled the 'best' china, cutlery, and linen serviettes in readiness to set the table. Within minutes, cloths were spread over the rich timber, and sprigs of ivy intertwined with tinsel completed the decoration down the centre.

Ten adults and four children squeezed around the table, leaving little room for anything but the best of manners—for the adults anyway.

Dawn paused to admire their handiwork before lowering her eyes while Harry said grace.

"Amen." Dawn glanced at her father-in-law, marvelling at the likeness between him and John. A little shorter, considerably less hair, and a few more wrinkles were all that discerned who was who—

unlike John's brothers, who shared similarities with Alice.

While bowls of vegetables and platters of meat were handed around the table, she took stock of her other Christmas companions.

Baby Richard, perched in the old wooden highchair, bashed his spoon on the tray, splattering mashed vegetables everywhere and chortling with delight. His mother, Jill, frowned at his two older brothers, Mark and Jack, as they wrestled over the wishbone from the roast chicken while the boys' father, Tim, seemed oblivious, raising his voice in conversation with Harry and making no attempt to quell the fight. Across the table, John's eldest brother, George, sat stiffly beside his perfectly groomed wife, Susan. Flanked by their son, Paul, and daughter, Cara, he was staring in obvious distaste at his nephews' behaviour and Dawn bit back a grin. Dressed formally, Paul wore a white shirt and tie, and Cara, a red and white crimplene dress with her hair piled in a topknot. It was hard to tell how old they were. *Ten and twelve?*

Unease wormed its way inside Dawn as her gaze locked on her mother, stiffly clutching her serviette in one hand. She was seated between Harry and an older gentleman who'd been introduced as the legendary Ed. Next to his enormous shoulders and significant height, Lillian appeared almost doll-like. Lillian's eyes were wide, her lips pursed, and she met Dawn's stare as the room evolved into what she knew her mother would describe later as 'pandemonium'. Dawn clenched her teeth to prevent the laughter than was threatening to burst out. For Dawn, the happy and chaotic mess of family, conversation, and love was exactly as she had always dreamed it should be—and what she had wanted all her life.

Having met John's siblings only once before, on the day of their wedding, Dawn realised suddenly how little she knew his family. Had her own adjustment to rural life prevented her from absorbing the snippets of information Alice had shared? Or had she been too self-absorbed to listen? She wracked her brain as she studied Susan's elegance and quiet demeanour before swivelling her gaze to her other sister-in-law. Jill's clear, makeup-free eyes wore a look of defeat and Dawn's heart went out to her. She could only imagine how hectic life must be with three little boys, even if her husband was as easy-going as John said he was. Jill smiled at Dawn, and her face softened before she was once again distracted by the baby.

Dawn's attention was interrupted as the bowl of roast vegetables reached her, and she concentrated on serving herself before handing it on.

She poured gravy over her meat and lifted her gaze once more, meeting the pale blue eyes of the eldest brother in the family, George. Quickly swivelling away from his stare, she looked toward Jill while her thoughts remained on him. *Are you checking on my manners? Or are you just being friendly?* She had been reminded of George's accounting competency when she'd asked John if they could buy the new lounge curtains. It seemed that in spite of no longer having a physical interest in the farm, he was accepted as both financial advisor and farm accountant, doing his best to control both his brother's and parents' expenditure. Alice had said they lived in Remuera, one of the poshest suburbs of Auckland, and, while the children attended the best possible schools and played sport during the weekends, Susan entertained the wives of her husband's acquaintances and business partners.

Jill could not have been more different. Honey coloured hair swung in wild curls around her flushed face, and her cotton dress was already covered with grubby marks and smeared vegetables from the baby's activities.

"Can I do anything to help?" Dawn asked her, laying her knife and fork neatly on the edge of her plate as she attempted to stand.

"No." Jill flapped her hand. "Eat your meal. We're fine." She chuckled and shook her head. "They're not usually quite this bad, but Christmas is an exciting time for them. As soon as they've eaten, they'll go outside and peace will reign."

Dawn smiled as Alice's words came back to her. Tim and Jill lived on a few acres on the outskirts of town, a short drive from where Tim was employed by the Kaipara Dairy Factory. Dawn regretted not getting to know her better before now and was sorry she hadn't been able to make it to Alice's morning tea.

Perhaps soon, I'll be pregnant and can share something more in common with her.

It was more than half an hour later before the plates were collected and the Christmas pudding served. Further arguments between the little boys dominated the conversation.

"He got a threepence and I didn't." Jack's lip quivered as he studied the pudding-covered silver treasure that Mark had extracted from his mouth.

Dawn bit into a coin and quickly held it up. "Here you are. One for you too. We'll give them a wash and you can take them home."

"Thanks." Jill smiled at Dawn and rolled her eyes.

A few minutes later, the jewel in the crown, the one and only sixpence, was located in the slab of pudding on Ed's plate. He held it silently aloft.

"My turn. It appears next year will be a lucky one for me," he said.

For me too I hope? She smiled at him.

———

With Christmas dinner over, Dawn volunteered to help Alice and Susan clear up while the others played cricket with the children.

"Paul will organise the little ones, and Cara can help Jill with the baby." Susan had graciously offered, appearing to ignore the glare her children gave her and their reluctance to leave the house. "Or, if you prefer, you can wash and dry the dishes."

Dawn bit back a chuckle and wordlessly plunged her rubber-gloved hands into the hot suds, methodically washing each and every item of crockery and cutlery. While Alice covered leftovers and put away as much as possible, Dawn wished she had thought to bring the new apron her mother had made her. Instead she'd donned the faded floral version that hung on the back of Alice's pantry door.

Susan's perfect lipstick, her glossy dark hair, teased and lacquered into a faultless French roll, and her plain cream shift dress with its mandarin collar, had unnerved Dawn to begin with. However, by the time the kitchen was neat and tidy, she suspected she had underestimated her sister-in-law. A quiet reserve seemed to hide an educated, friendly woman.

Susan allowed a long sigh to escape. "Phew. I thought we had a lot of dishes to wash in our house – but nothing like the amount here."

Dawn grinned at her. "I'll carry the glasses if you like. You bring the lemonade."

Susan returned her smile, picked up the jug, and followed her out into the sunshine.

Under the shade of the puriri tree, a circle of garden chairs and a long timber bench provided seating for the group of family and friends to lounge away the afternoon, sipping cool lemonade or joining the children and men in their own version of cricket.

———

"DID YOU ENJOY YOUR FIRST CHRISTMAS ON FANTAIL Ridge?" John whispered in Dawn's ear as they snuggled in bed late that night.

She hesitated for a moment, revelling in the softness of his skin as she stroked his upper arm.

"I did, actually." She was surprised. "It was more enjoyable than I had expected. I didn't think I'd have anything in common with Susan or Jill, but I liked them both, and I hope we can become firm friends." She spoke softly, aware of her mother in the next room. "I'm not sure if Mum enjoyed her day, but it had to have been better than her sitting at home with only the radio and perhaps one of her bridge friends for company."

He wrapped his arms around her and held her tight. "I'm sorry your Christmas present didn't arrive on time. We'll go into town after New Year's as I'm sure it will be here by then."

Dawn's interest was heightened. He would not give away any hints. Whatever the gift was, she knew it must be something big. She grinned in the dark as her thoughts flew to George's solemn face, and she wondered how much trouble John had gone to in order to get permission to buy whatever it was.

"I like my gumboots," she said and laughed softly. "You might pretend to be a tough farmer, but you're really a very thoughtful romantic at heart, aren't you?"

He chuckled quietly and brushed the hair from her face before lifting his head to kiss her.

———

"I'D LIKE TO GO HOME TODAY PLEASE."

Dawn stared at her mother, her forehead wrinkling. "I thought you were staying until after the New Year's dance?"

Lillian sniffed and dropped her shoulders. "I've stayed long enough. I know where you live now, and I've met John's family. It's time for me to return to my own world and not waste any more time." She finished by crossing her arms and facing Dawn, as though daring her to challenge her decision.

"Alright, Mum. If that's what you wish, I'll check with John, and we'll take you to the station in time to catch the two o'clock train."

A sliver of concern wormed its way into her, wrestling with guilty relief. She understood that neither she nor her mother had been born country women—but Lillian hadn't even tried to fit in. She had refused to touch the cat or go near the coop sitting on the back lawn containing a bantam hen and eight tiny chickens. With the exception of short walks around the house paddock and out to the road and back, she had sat in the sun, read, played solitary card games, and occasionally dried the evening dishes. That was all—and Dawn had despaired.

While leaning back in her seat as they drove towards Helensville, memories danced in Dawn's mind. Studying her mother's profile, sitting bolt upright in the front, she squirmed in surprise. She had lived on the farm for four months, and in all that time, her own behaviour had been frighteningly similar to her mother's.

A knot formed deep inside her, and she rubbed the back of her neck and focused on the tight curls at the back of John's head and the lines fanning from the edges of his eyes. He caught her gaze in the rear-vision mirror and grinned. Her heart surged as heat rose to her cheeks. His tolerance, patience, and gentle understanding had been unwavering, and the thought of living without him didn't bear thinking about.

She would try harder. Perhaps she could become a country woman after all.

CHAPTER 8

Vehicles lined the grass verge as the sun began to set, spreading a soft golden glow on the horizon and blending with the welcoming lights of the hall.

Dawn stepped out of the car cautiously, her high heels sinking into the soft ground. Her nerves jangled and she gratefully tucked her hand into John's. Was she ready for these community gatherings? It had been a big adjustment settling into the wide open spaces, coupled with the expectations of farm life. The loss of her own identity after years in the salon hit her. Here she was no longer Dawn Burton, the vivacious young hairdresser from *A Cut Ahead*. She was simply Dawn, wife of John Simpson.

"Hello there! Lovely to see you again, Dawn."

The cheery voice came from Bev, her dark-haired neighbour who was striding towards them and towing her tall, slender husband behind her. She wore a scarlet floral dress, tightly nipped in the waist with a full skirt that swung around her knees. Like Dawn, her feet were thrust into court shoes, her hair teased and held in place with spray. She extended her hands and clasped Dawn's, her wide smile lighting her face.

"You probably don't recognise my husband, Charlie." She laughed and indicated the man standing behind her.

Dawn met the green eyes set in a round, weatherbeaten face and took his outstretched hand. His spotless white shirt and black trousers contrasted with his shock of red hair and thick beard.

"Hello again." A thread of humour dominated his deep voice and she smiled.

"Hello," Dawn said as Bev released Dawn's hand and hooked her arm through Dawn's.

"Come with me. I'll introduce you around."

Dawn's eyes widened as she looked back at John. He shrugged, a gentle smile on his face, and turned his attention to Charlie.

The porch led to a pair of doors that opened into a medium-sized hall lined with wooden seats along each wall and a stage at the end, supporting a band. A chord struck as the women entered. Dawn jumped as a drum roll was joined by the saxophone and pianist playing the startling opening of Neil Sedaka's 'Breaking Up is Hard to Do'.

Small groups milled around, and Bev swept Dawn past them and into the kitchen off the side of the main room. Dawn ogled the trestle tables loaded with sandwiches, slices, cakes, and a wide range of savouries—enough to feed a hundred or more. *So this is country catering. I don't think we needed a meal before we came.*

Introductions were made and for a few minutes, Dawn squirmed at the inquisitive eyes boring into her from every direction. Unable to remember a single person's name, she smiled anxiously and pushed a lock of hair behind her ear that had determinedly escaped its lacquered prison. The band progressed through a series of fast, modern songs, and couples filled the floor.

She glanced around, desperately seeking John, and breathed a sigh of relief as she felt his hand envelop hers. He swung her around to face him and launched into a jive, guiding her back and forth under his arm and around the floor. Within minutes, she was giddy with both exertion and happiness. He was a good dancer, confidently leading her through a cha-cha and samba, and then twisting wildly with her to the increased tempo of the music.

People continued to pour through the door, including Alice and Harry, both bearing many plates of food. By the time the band took a break and Dawn allowed John to lead her to a seat, not only the dance floor, but the kitchen and porch were spilling over with a wide range of farmers, wives, children, and friends. Someone threw the windows open, and Dawn stared into the inky night. Outside, glass bottles clinked and a group shouted 'cheers'. Dawn swallowed. *I could handle a cold drink.*

There didn't appear to be a bar, and she leaned into John. "I'm thirsty."

He pulled her to her feet and guided her into the kitchen where jugs of cordial were set out on one of the tables. She looked at him, her head inclined and one eyebrow raised.

"Yes, I'm afraid so. A few of the blokes bring beer, but strictly speaking, cordial is the drink of the day. This is considered a family event, and the committee don't allow alcohol inside the hall."

She nodded and accepted the glass of red liquid he handed her. Sculling one himself, he placed the cup on the tray of empties and waited while Dawn finished hers. The band struck up again, this time with slower, romantic music.

"Come on. It's the ballroom dances next." He wrapped his arm around her waist and led her through the door as couples positioned themselves in a circle.

As the emcee announced the Valeta Waltz, Dawn breathed a sigh of relief. She had rarely been allowed to attend dances, however, a high school music teacher had instructed her students in the basic and most popular dance steps. Dawn and Ann had made good use of the empty music room in Ann's parents' home, turning the record player up and practicing at every opportunity. The only downfall had been learning the dances while each clutched a broom—not quite the same as having a partner to dance with. Now, Dawn had to concentrate hard to keep in time with John and not trip over his feet.

At nine-thirty on the dot, the band stopped playing, and the lead singer announced supper was ready.

John guided her to the queue forming in the doorway and introduced her to yet more locals while they waited their turn to load a plate, collect a drink, and find a seat. He was a gracious and attentive partner, and a surge of love for him ran through Dawn's veins.

"Does Ed come to these things?" Dawn glanced around the crowd, trying to remember names and find familiar faces.

"No, never. He's not very social. Never has been. I'll tell you more about him on the way home. It's a bit noisy here." He gave her a rueful smile, and she nodded in agreeance.

As the noise level escalated, she took the opportunity to slip out the side door to the toilets. She had barely closed the door behind her when someone entered the room and low voices penetrated the thin wall.

"I've heard she behaves like a proper little madam. Puts poor Harry and Alice through hell—after all they've done for her. And John is such a gorgeous soul. So kind, and he worships the ground she walks on."

Dawn froze as a second, more gentle voice responded.

"I've heard a few locals say she's a good hairdresser though. Apparently very pleasant. Perhaps she's been taught she has to be if she wants to keep customers … or maybe she's a different person in her own world."

Doors slammed, followed soon after by water running, but it was another five minutes before Dawn could be sure she was alone. She opened the door, cast a furtive glance around her, and slipped back into the hall, surveying the crowd.

Shame twisted in her gut, her confidence crushed by the overheard whispers. The revelation of other's opinions shocked her to the core—and the reality of the words bit hard. *Have I been that bad?* She shook her head slightly and her stomach tightened. It seemed that someone in the district thought so—or could it be sour grapes? She might be new to the district but she was certain of one thing. Disparaging comments would not have come from within the family. Her memory darted back to Alice's morning tea and the unpleasant encounter with Mrs Harris, the well-known gossip. *Argh, I wonder?*

She drew a breath and pressed against the wall, willing it to swallow her. Charlie and Bev were nearby, talking to a group of young people with their backs to her. She slunk past them, not wanting to risk inclusion, and watched Alice make her way slowly along the row of seated attendees, carrying a massive teapot. It was clear she was offering a top up to those who precariously balanced cups and saucers on their knees. Other than that, the only person she could remember the name of was a young woman of a similar age to herself, introduced by Bev as another newlywed relatively new on the peninsula, Carol. Did Bev and Charlie also think she behaved like a spoilt brat?

Dawn's gaze rested on Carol for a few moments. Unlike most, she appeared to be without a partner, squeezed between an elderly couple and staring into the crowd. She was thin, with dark rings under her eyes, contrasting with her bright lipstick. She wore a full skirt of pale blue and a white blouse with a stain down one sleeve, as though someone had already spilled a drink over her. Something about her expression drew sympathy from deep within Dawn. Did she also feel like an outsider? Dawn wished she were better at forming friendships. *Lord knows, I need all I can get.*

At five minutes before midnight, everyone crossed their arms in front of them and joined hands with their neighbour, forming a circle around the perimeter of the dance floor. Dawn found herself clasping Carol's hand, and she gave her a warm smile. As time was counted down, everyone moved rhythmically toward the centre and back out again while the drummer beat time to the chanting. On the dot of twelve, an all-encompassing cheer sounded and the band struck up with Auld Lang Syne. As they swayed and sang, Dawn gripped John's hand on one side and Carol's small, thin fingers more firmly on the other, allowing determination to flow into her as new resolutions formed.

Another woman in similar circumstances to me. I hope we can become friends.

———

THEY WERE ALMOST HOME BEFORE DAWN REMEMBERED her earlier question.

"Tell me about Ed, John? What happened to the wharf?"

He took his eyes off the road for a second to glance at her. "It's gone now. Rotted and floated away probably. Used to be next to the beach in the inlet between Charlie and Bev's and our paddock, across the road from home. The shack was moved to his farm after he came back from the war."

"Keep going," she urged.

"I told you he grew up in Norway. Apparently, he worked on a ship that was wrecked off the west coast back in 1921. Mum and Dad didn't know his story for years because he'd lost his memory and didn't have a clue where he came from. Then he had an accident and was concussed—and his memory returned. Dad helped him get citizenship before he went to war."

Dawn shuffled upright. "I wonder why he never married. There was no shortage of women around who would have been happy to live on the land with a good-looking Nordic man." She couldn't forget her own transition issues and an ache of empathy sat deep within her.

"He was in his forties by the time he settled and has been pretty busy turning that rough country into the nice dairy farm and piggery he has. Anyway, he's very reclusive, so I suppose he's content with his own company."

John squeezed her hand again as he drove over the cattle grid at their boundary. "Tell you what—I'll take you to his place for a visit soon. You'll like it. His house is the same as ours but has a huge garden around it, and flowers and vegetables all the way out to the road. He also has a big aviary between the house and cowshed where he nurses all sorts of injured native birds until they're well enough to be released."

An hour later, Dawn lay awake, oblivious to John's warm, regular breaths against her neck as she mulled over the crushing comments she'd overheard and the life Ed may have had before coming to South Head. A Morepork hooted outside, its mournful call reminding her that a new year had begun—one in which she was determined to meet the challenges that she faced and improve the relationships she had so obviously made a mess of.

CHAPTER 9

"Is it really for me?" Disbelief, excitement, and a touch of anxiety welled inside her. She ran her hand over the bonnet of the little cream Morris Minor. John's sudden and urgent need to pop over to talk to Charlie about something late on the previous afternoon now made sense. *Charlie must have picked it up to help with the surprise.*

"Of course it's for you. I'm sorry it wasn't here for Christmas."

She swung around and hugged John.

He took her hand and escorted her to the driver's door. "Hop in. See what you think."

She slid onto the red leather seat and stroked the steering wheel gently. A smile tipped the corners of her mouth, widening as she adjusted the rear-view mirror before studying the knobs and levers.

John strode around the car to the passenger seat

and, one by one, explained the functions. "Before you turn a corner, you must indicate by flicking this lever. Up if you're turning left and down if you're going right."

Dawn gripped both hands on the wheel, her knuckles shining white.

"Don't worry. A couple of trips around the paddock and up and down to Mum and Dad's and you'll have the hang of it. Once you do, we'll drive into town, and you can sit your licence."

Tentatively and with a few initial hiccups, Dawn spent the next hour see-sawing between tension and elation as she adjusted to the vehicle and its idiosyncrasies.

"Are you ready to drive to Mum and Dad's?"

Dawn took a deep breath and squared her shoulders. "Why not?"

She changed gears and manoeuvred the little car across the paddock and over the grid. With growing confidence, she braked at the road edge, flicked the indicator, and giggled as the red flag-like lever popped out of the strut between the front and back doors and stood horizontally, pointing in the direction they intended to head.

With no other traffic on the road and her window down, she changed gears as frequently as possible, and accelerated to a speed that allowed the breeze to catch her hair and lift it from her neck. Negotiating the entrance to the Fantail Ridge yard, she plunged the clutch to the floor, changed down, and halted neatly outside the house gate.

"Well done." John reached over and kissed her cheek before throwing his door open and hurrying to her side of the car.

Alice was in the front garden and came to meet them, her faded apron tied firmly around her waist, and her gumboots covered in fresh dirt. Her cheeks were pink, and her wide smile reached her eyes. "Congratulations. Look at you. Next thing we know, you'll be in charge of the farm truck."

Dawn laughed. "I doubt it, but thanks for the confidence." She pushed the gate open and stopped abruptly as her cardigan caught on the edge of the sign. "Oh. Hang on a second. Fantail Ridge has nabbed me." She unhooked the thread and stepped back, studying the sign for a moment. "Where did the name *Fantail Ridge* come from? Are there many fantails around?"

"John. Don't tell me you haven't even taken Dawn to see the fantails yet?" Alice turned to Dawn and raised an eyebrow. "I named the farm soon after we came here." She pointed to the thick native bush that lined the southern side of the house yard. "There's a track through there that leads down to the flat and, especially in spring and summer, the fantails are prolific. They nest in its shelter and, I suppose because there are so many insects that also live in the bush, it's a great hunting ground for them."

Dawn shot John a glance and he gave her a rueful

smile and shrugged. "It's always been Mum's 'thing'. I'll take you for a walk through there one day."

"You know what, Dawn? I'll take you myself right now." Alice hauled off her apron and draped it over John's shoulder. "You can go and find your father. He's down in the woolshed cleaning up now that the truck has finally been to collect the bales from last November's shearing. We'll be back in half an hour for a cuppa."

Grasping Dawn by the elbow, Alice urged her toward the house paddock. Dawn gave John a wave and strode along with her mother-in-law. Within minutes, they had reached the overgrown trail, and Dawn held Alice's arm as they picked their way down the steep slope. At the bottom, the track opened out onto a wider pathway and flattened slightly.

"Stop and listen." Alice grabbed Dawn's hand, and they paused for a minute. "There's one."

Dawn followed Alice's pointed finger as a small brown and yellow bird flitted back and forth across the track only a few feet from where they stood.

Resuming a slower pace, they strolled on, delight and fascination filling Dawn's soul. Alice was a good guide, pointing out nests of other birds as well as the fantails, and the various native trees and plants. The cool, green environment nurtured a sense of peace and tranquillity within Dawn.

"I can see why you enjoy coming for walks through here," Dawn said.

Alice shrugged. "I do. I love this bush as much as I love my park, but I don't come as often as I used to." She stood still and took a couple of slow breaths. "To be honest, I don't think I'm as fit as I used to be."

Dawn frowned and she reached out with a stab of concern. "Here, take my arm. Perhaps we'd better head back now and have that cup of tea."

Alice chuckled as Dawn slipped her arm into Alice's. "I'm not totally incapacitated yet—but I think we will walk back up via the road. It's not as pretty but at least it's not so steep."

By the time they reached the top of hill, even Dawn was puffing, and she laughed. "I hope that husband of mine has got morning tea ready. I'm gasping for a cuppa."

———

THE FOLLOWING WEEKEND, EAGER TO HAVE MORE driving practice before she faced her test, Dawn suggested John accompany her to visit Ed. The telephone had finally been connected to their house and, in spite of Ed's reclusiveness, she had been astounded when their first call had been a thirty-second invitation from him to visit for afternoon tea—and to cut his hair.

Soon after lunch, she settled the basket containing chocolate patty cakes on the back seat, stowed her hairdressing bag and gumboots in the rear, and slid behind the steering wheel.

Although recently graded and relatively free of corrugations, the road was covered with loose gravel, making it slippery. A trail of dust followed the car as Dawn negotiated the steep sections and sharp turns that commanded every skerrick of her attention.

"We're coming up to Ed's entrance now, so slow down and prepare," John said.

Following his instructions, she crept the vehicle along the fence line beside a row of pine trees until the driveway opened out to a swath of green kikuyu grass edged with a cottage garden awash with shrubs, flowers, and an assortment of herbs and vegetables.

"Wow!" She braked directly in front of a five-barred timber gate.

"Yes. It certainly is wow," John agreed. "Might as well pull over on the grass there and turn her off. We'll walk from here."

After collecting the basket and hair-cutting kit, Dawn followed John through the gate and picked her way across the stepping stones toward the white house, a carbon copy of their own.

A small table rested on the lawn surrounded by three wooden chairs and covered with a checked tablecloth.

"Hello there."

At the sound of Ed's deep voice, she jerked her head up and met his welcoming smile.

"I love your garden, Ed." Dawn couldn't think what else to say. Everywhere she looked, the farm and garden bloomed with love and attention, and in the summer sun, a wide range of colourful flowers, of every height and width, leaned against the house wall, distracting her from the austere boredom of the plain exterior. "Your house is the same as ours, but not as ugly."

John chuckled and a gentle smile played around Ed's mouth as he responded.

"Thank you. You forget that I have had many years to make this a home. In time, and perhaps with some seeds and cuttings from myself and others, you will also love yours. It's not the house that makes a home; it's the love and tolerance within it."

Dawn stared into the older man's deep blue eyes. She was tall for a woman but under his penetrating gaze, she shrank as his comments resonated with her. *Has he also formed a poor impression of me?* She felt as small as a mouse, and time seemed to stand still. Her gaze slipped from Ed's wrinkled, nut-brown face, his head topped with a mop of unruly thick grey hair, to his faded tartan shirt and khaki trousers, and down to the huge, muddied boots.

She had no memory of her own father, but something about Ed reminded Dawn of a sepia photo her mother had on the dressing table in her bedroom. It was not the clothing—her dad was in military dress—but rather the way they shared a similar stance, tall and proud, with no hint of age or injury.

"Would you like to have tea first, or have a look around?" Ed asked.

Dawn looked towards John, meekly seeking guidance.

"I think Dawn's interested in seeing your birds, Ed," John replied.

"Very well then. Perhaps you'd like to change your shoes and then follow me?"

Dawn smiled and returned to the car to collect her boots.

———

THE AVIARY COVERED AN AREA AS LARGE AS THE AVERAGE city house yard, and appreciation of the affinity Ed had for animals grew rapidly within Dawn. A hen pheasant with a badly broken wing rested quietly amongst the internal forested area within the enclosure while two Moreporks attempted to hide in the tree limbs above them. A magpie hopped across the ground and Ed stooped and put his hand down, allowing the bird to climb up his arm onto his shoulder.

"I think this little one will be with me a while yet. There's nothing wrong with him, but he was only a baby when I found him injured on the side of the road."

"Will he ever be free again?" Dawn frowned as concern filled her.

"Yes. As he becomes less reliant on me for food, I

will let him out each day. Then, when he feels ready to become fully independent, he can."

A Tui flew across the aviary, stopping to rest on a branch at eye level. It tipped its head back and a melodious song burst from its throat, the white feathers under his neck bobbing in harmony.

A smile spread across Dawn's face. "Isn't it beautiful? I've never seen a Tui so close before."

Ed turned to her and grinned. "Their song is very musical. This one is nearly ready for release—his broken leg is mending well, so this will probably be his last week in captivity."

Dawn raised her eyebrows. She had never thought about wild animals or birds. What would happen if people like Ed didn't help them? Would they just die? Are they being injured because of humans taking over their natural habitat? Questions swirled in her head as she considered the complexities of nature for the first time in her life.

"Would you like to come and see the piggery now?" Ed asked.

John answered before she had a chance to open her mouth. "Definitely. Last time I was here you were building extra yards for the sows."

They followed Ed out of the aviary and waited while he latched the door behind them. A black and white dog lay outside a kennel nearby, and Ed walked over and unclipped its chain. It sprang away to a nearby tree and squatted, its tongue lolling cheerfully.

Dawn's experience with farm animals had been limited to viewing a few cows and sheep out of the train windows when they passed pockets of rural land, or on the few occasions she and Ann had packed a picnic and taken it to Cornwall Park.

She stared at the pig enclosure, wrinkling her nose as they drew closer and picking her way carefully along the concrete path. A squeal followed by a series of snorts emanated from the low building, and she clutched John's arm. He took her hand and squeezed it reassuringly.

"Don't be nervous. I'm here with you."

As her eyes adjusted to the darkened interior, she noticed lamps in the corner of each pen, under which sat a large box filled with straw.

"This is the nursery." Ed reached into one of the boxes and removed a tiny pink squirming piglet. He held the creature out toward Dawn, and she drew back before tentatively stroking its head with a finger. It made soft grunting sounds and tried to snuffle into her hand.

"You can hold it—like this." Ed gently took her arm and folded it across her body before placing the piglet on it and covering it with her other hand. "Keep it warm. They feel the cold, especially when they're so small."

An unfamiliar emotion seeped into her, similar to when Poppy was on her lap, purring. *Is this what motherhood would feel like?*

The piglet turned its face toward hers, and her chest burst with love. "It's very sweet. Are they all this little?"

"No." Ed smiled and inclined his head. "Follow me."

She walked a few steps farther on, halted beside the big man and gazed into each of the six pens. Every one contained a litter of babies accompanied by an enormous mother. Dawn was astounded at the size of the sows—in most cases, considerably bigger than a sheep, but with shorter legs.

"Do they go outside?" she asked.

Ed pointed to a small doorway on the opposite side. "Yes, through there. Each pen has its own yard so the mothers can go in and out as they wish. When the piglets are big enough, they also join them, and when it's hot, there are cool mud wallows out there for them to bathe in."

"Oh." Dawn studied them for a long minute before handing the piglet back. Her astonishment compounded the realisation of how little she had been exposed to in her life and something deep inside her blossomed.

With the baby back in the box with its siblings, Ed turned to head back the way they had come. He waved toward the concrete troughs than ran alongside each pen. "That's where I put their milk and vegetables each morning and night. Fresh water runs through the pipe along the back, and they access it through those special nozzles."

Dawn studied the set-up, her admiration for Ed

growing. Accustomed now to the odour, she searched for the source, surprised to note how spotless the entire dwelling was.

"What is that smell?" She couldn't help herself and was taken aback when both John and Ed laughed.

"It's the pig toilet," John explained.

She frowned and tilted her head questioningly.

"Pigs are very clean and like to use the same place for toileting. However, it does get a bit smelly, especially when it's warm and the wind is blowing this way, as it is today. Every day, I clean the pens and pile the manure up for use in the gardens and paddocks."

Dawn looked at John, narrowing her eyes. "So … is that instead of that horrible grey powdery stuff you and your dad spread all over the place at home?"

Ed interjected, explaining quietly and clearly. "I prefer to use natural methods for all my farming and gardening. It's the way I grew up and the amount produced here by the pigs and cows provides me with more than enough. I have no need to purchase any of the new products or chemicals."

John grinned at her before facing Ed. "Dawnie's got a lot to learn about farming. Mum and Dad never used chemicals—except sheep dip—either, but it's the sixties now, and we have so many options available to make farming easier and more efficient."

Dawn turned back to the contented animals she'd just met and allowed herself to dwell on the situation. *I think I agree with Ed. Why spend money on artificial products when he can use what is produced here?*

By the time they had walked past the paddock of jersey cows, contentedly grazing on the summer grass, and headed back to the lawn for afternoon tea and chocolate cakes, loneliness, the critical comments from unknown neighbours, and her old life in the city had disappeared from her mind.

CHAPTER 10

Dawn drove slowly, concentrating on the road as the sun lowered and flashed across the windscreen, distracting her at every western turn.

She flicked the sun visor down and gripped the wheel fiercely. Barely a word was spoken before she pulled up outside their house and breathed a long sigh. "Phew. Made it."

"You did really well, love. Did you enjoy your afternoon?" Concern crept into John's voice, and she shot him a grin.

"I did. Actually, I enjoyed it much more than I expected to. Ed seems kind of ... like a mix of some kind of distant relative and one of those ... conservationists. He's a really interesting person." She stopped and quietly contemplated the patience he had shown and the answers he had provided to her many—and probably naïve—questions. "I'm glad he said I could come any time because I just might do that. If nothing else, that thick mop of hair he has needs a regular trim."

She reached into the back seat for the empty basket and closed the door behind her.

"What's for tea?"

Dawn laughed. "Are you really hungry already, even after those three cakes you ate at afternoon tea?"

"Of course. That was two hours ago—almost."

Dawn giggled as John pushed the gate open. "It's sausages, veggies and gravy."

"Yum. My favourite." John smiled as Poppy wound herself around his legs, meowing. He bent and picked her up before handing her to Dawn. "I'll let the dogs off for a run and feed them while you get it started."

As Dawn cuddled the cat in her arms, John walked towards the clump of trees on the far side of the garage with Sandy, the younger of the two dogs, bounding along beside him. Alice and Harry had finally ventured off on their long-awaited cruise and, although they would only be absent for three weeks, John had relocated the working dogs from the homestead to new kennels a short distance from the chook pen. Each day when Dawn fed the chickens, she forced herself to take another step closer to them, speaking to them as though they were her best friends. Gyp would thrash her tail wildly against the wooden floor, while Sandy studied her with pricked ears and Dawn gradually gained more confidence. Without John knowing, she had reached out the previous day and stroked Gyp's head gently. Her coat was soft and silky under her hand and the dog seemed to understand her fear, making no attempt to invade her personal space or jump on her. Sandy was more enthusiastic, and Dawn guiltily gave him a wide berth unless John was around to discipline him.

Walking slowly inside, Dawn thought about the photo that sat proudly on the office desk in Harry and Alice's home.

A replica of Gyp had stared out of the frame at her —a black and tan Huntaway—and when Dawn had asked Alice about the dog, she'd picked up the timber frame and stroked it gently as she told the story of the mysterious canine that had followed the boys home when John was a young child. They had called her Flossie and loved her dearly for seventeen years. She was Gyp's grandmother, and together, Flossie and Rock, the sandy-coloured bitser that had proved to be Harry's faithful companion, had provided the foundation stock of working dogs that now assisted so many of their friends and neighbours on their farms. Flossie and Rock were buried in Alice's 'park', the steep triangular area of land filled with trees and bulbs that hugged the hill between the road and the patch of native bush below the homestead.

A seat overlooking the park appeared to be the family's go-to place for rare minutes of relaxation and quiet conversation. Adjacent to the bench, two small white crosses rested side by side. Presumably there had been other dogs that had worked and died on Fantail Ridge before Sandy and Gyp were born, but Dawn had been privy to hearing only about Flossie and Rock.

She looked down at Poppy. Her eyes were closed and a rhythmic purr emanated from her little grey body. Dawn leaned her cheek against her fur, and the strange ache she'd felt when she held the piglet once again dominated her soul.

Love is such a beautiful, exciting feeling.

———

DURING MOST OF JANUARY, HAY-MAKING TOOK precedence over any other farm chore, and for the first time since coming to Fantail Ridge, Dawn looked across the golden fields and realised that the dread of wide open spaces and a deep-seated need to be loved had faded. Here, there was room to breathe, run, and just be.

Too busy to think about her homesickness for the city, Dawn followed Alice's written instructions to the letter. She provided meals for John and the assorted friends and neighbours who turned up to help, relishing the importance of her new role. Tim, Jill, and the boys spent days at the farm before school resumed, making the most of a holiday while enjoying the use of the vacant homestead.

"Mike's coming to help us." Dawn had stared at

John blankly when he hung up the phone and relayed the information a few days earlier.

"Mike. Who's he?"

"You know. The new farm scheme fellow."

Dawn nodded, relieved they would have another strong pair of hands to help.

Harry had mentioned the scheme in a random conversation one Sunday and Dawn had listened intently at the time, astounded at the cooperative manner in which the community had resolved the shortage of casual labour. With a grant from the government, a removal house had been purchased and installed on the piece of land donated by one of the farmers in the area. Everyone else had joined forces in fencing the block, building a garage, and setting up a booking system and pay rate. Any one of them could employ the worker when extra labour was needed and the invoice was paid by the employer. With organisation—and the occasional disgruntled concession when more than one farm needed him at the same time—the scheme worked well, keeping the man in regular work throughout the year.

With Tim operating the tractor and baler and Mike driving the truck, John, and the neighbour from the south side of Fantail Ridge, Hugh Bennett, grasped the bales as they chugged up the conveyor chain then stacked them in neat rows on the vehicle's tray. As the layers grew, Dawn's apprehension increased. Were the men too busy to notice that the top bales were teetering precariously?

Eventually, John and Hugh had nowhere left to stand and thumped on the cab roof, yelling, "Full load!"

Back at the hayshed, she and Jill laid out food and drinks on a rug while the men transferred the hay into the shed, forming a neat jigsaw puzzle of stacks and pausing only when the truck was empty and it was time to return for the next load.

Having finally overcome her fear of the dogs, Dawn smiled as they romped and trotted alongside her. Accompanied by the children, she rolled the bales of hay from their haphazard exit from the baler onto the ground, while Jill took the empty food containers back to the house. The neat, straight rows of compressed blocks of dry grass made easy work for the truck and loader to sweep up the conveyor belt. Gyp seemed to understand Dawn's growing respect for the dogs and placed herself quietly at her feet at every opportunity, allowing the love between them to grow.

When the hay fields eventually stood empty, their golden stalks were quickly overcome with new green shoots and the cycle began again. First the horses were allowed into the paddock to graze, followed by cattle, and lastly, the sheep, who preferred the short, fresh blades of grass.

As summer drew to an end and showers once again blew in from the sea, Dawn stood in front of the mirror and studied her thin figure. She was fit, tanned —and healthier than she had ever been.

———

AUTUMN CAME EARLY, THE LEAVES ON THE MAPLE IN Alice's park yellowing and blending with the stalky seed heads of the grass below it.

Dawn drew her jacket tightly across her chest and glanced towards the house for the umpteenth time. Her mouth curved upwards, one foot tapping urgently against the leg of the wooden garden seat as the doctor's words replayed in her head.

"Congratulations. You're going to be a mother. I can hear a heartbeat."

Filled with delight and relief, she'd almost hugged the kindly man, instead throwing him her widest smile, and allowing her mind to drift. She barely heard his comments, noting only that the baby would be due in spring, before rushing out the door and leaping into her car. With her foot pressed as hard as she dared, she urged the little Morris up the hills and flew along the flats at twice her normal speed.

John's truck was parked outside the homestead, and she drew to a halt behind it. She hesitated before getting out, wanting to tell him her news before sharing it with his parents. However, getting him on his own was never easy during the day. Not for the first time, guilt stabbed at her for the resentment she felt at the strong bond her husband had with his parents. She approached the shed with butterflies doing gymnastics in her stomach.

John's back faced her as he bent over the welder, seeming unaware of her presence.

"Hello, love." Harry was the first to see her approach, and she smiled at him before reaching out to touch John lightly on the shoulder. It took a few seconds before the sparks stopped flying and he raised the face mask and met her eyes.

She cupped her hand around his ear and pressed her face against his. "I need to tell you something. Can you meet me under the puriri tree?"

He nodded and pointed to the piece of steel held tightly in the vice in front of him. "I'll finish this and see you shortly."

While she waited, her excitement bubbled, and she relaxed and let reality set in. *My dream is coming true.* She bent her head and rubbed her stomach. *It won't be long and we'll be a proper family.*

Her mind wandered, and she started as the gate clicked behind her.

She stood and threw her arms around John before smoothing the wrinkles from his forehead with long, gentle fingers. "It's good news so you don't have to frown. We're going to be parents!"

He stood frozen for a few seconds, as though he couldn't understand what she was saying. His smile widened and he picked her up and swung her in a circle.

"That's fantastic news." Grasping her hand, he turned to the gate again. "Let's tell Mum and Dad."

Her delight overflowed as they ran toward the house, arriving breathless at the back door. Gyp lay on the mat and leapt to her feet, nudging Dawn's hand as though seeking an explanation for their abundant joy.

Alice dropped the tray of scones on the cooling rack and looked up as Dawn and John burst through the kitchen door. Harry flicked the newspaper closed and pushed himself out of the chair.

"You tell them." John's arm rested on Dawn's shoulder as the heat rose on her cheeks.

"You're going to be grandparents again." Dawn's voice rose with excitement as a wide beam spread across Alice's face.

"That's wonderful news." Alice hugged Dawn first before turning to her son. "I'd better get the knitting needles out again."

Harry squeezed Dawn gently, and she leaned against his prickly cheek. "Congratulations, love. We're overjoyed for you both."

Later that night, Dawn lay quietly, her hands folded over her stomach, listening to the rhythmic breaths of her husband. Disbelief alternated with anticipation and anxiety, and it was well into the night before she drifted into sleep.

CHAPTER 11

Squeezed between Alice and the passenger door while Harry drove the truck, Dawn swayed as they moved back and forth over the bumps. Diesel fumes rose from the struggling engine, and she swallowed the bile that rose in her throat.

"Stop please!" She threw the door open before the truck ground to a full halt and was violently ill. Wiping her mouth, she gulped lungs full of fresh air. She climbed back into the cab.

Alice patted her hand and smiled. "You'll feel better soon—and it's for a good cause."

Dawn shot her a wan grin and straightened her shoulders. She hadn't been sick for several days—and was less tired. However, perhaps a breakfast of lamb chops and eggs, mixed with the rough ride in the truck, was one step too far. The last thing she'd wanted to do was to plant marram grass and lupins, but it was either that or stay at home alone —again.

As the truck ground its way across the top of the ridge between the far corner of the home farm and the new property, the wind whistled through the open windows and Dawn immediately felt better. Spindrift blew in from the ocean, sending a haze across the sand dunes, and mixed with the thick, strappy clumps of toetoe and flax, softening the harshness of the cabbage trees that lined the coast.

Ahead of them, John drove the tractor, towing the newly modified planter he and Harry had been working on. Dawn had cross-questioned both Harry and John about the how and why of its operation, eager to correct improve her knowledge and understanding. She slumped in frustration. There seemed to be so much to learn about farming and almost none of it came with written instructions. She would not ask again, sure things would become clearer in time.

An hour later, while the four of them bent to inspect the samples of sandy soil John had taken, a gentle shower blew over, dampening the dust.

"Perfect. Let's get started," Harry called.

Alice led Dawn to the tiny metal seats at the front of the planter.

"You sit there, and I'll perch on this one. It's our job to fill the drills with marram seedlings."

Starting slowly, Harry allowed the vehicle to creep forward while Dawn copied Alice's rhythm. Bend, straighten, grab another bundle of seedlings, and drop them roots first into the soil. Her nausea disappeared and she was surprised how much she enjoyed the repetitious work. At the back of the planter, a long metal box was welded to the frame and, following the deposit of each slip of grass, a row of lupin seeds fell to the ground in a neatly measured pattern.

The tractor trundled back and forth along the edge of the sandy ridge, gradually working towards the rough grassland where flax bushes and trees grew randomly amongst the kikuyu. By mid-afternoon, the threatening clouds that had gradually become heavier unleashed their load, soaking the workers within minutes and burying the seed in the ground.

"Couldn't be better timing." John shook the rain off his jacket and stood closer to Dawn as they sheltered under a tree.

"I can't wait to see the lupins flower in spring," Alice said.

"Why did you have to plant them … and will they all be yellow like that one in the tub of daffodils was?" Dawn inclined her head as she directed her question to Alice.

"The flowers are not unlike delphiniums to look at, only they vary in colour. Mostly purples and pinks but they also come in yellow and blue. Remember? I mentioned they're helpful because they fix nitrogen in the soil and provide nutrients for other grasses to stabilise and grow—therefore providing nutritious food for the stock as well as the ground."

Dawn sighed. It seemed being pregnant really could affect your memory. She knew they were pretty but the scientific reason for planting them had completely slipped her mind. She nodded. "And the marram grass?"

"It's a tough, easy-to-grow grass that holds the sand together and stops erosion. I didn't know much about it before coming to South Head, but it's used widely around the coastlines in many countries, not just New Zealand," Harry added. "Another couple of days, and we'll have the area finished. Then we can think about building yards."

A tiny frown formed between Dawn's eyes. Farming certainly was a business—a much bigger one than she had ever realised. She placed a hand on her stomach, thinking of her growing child. *At least you will have security in the future.*

———

A week later, with the planting finished, John and Harry headed to the run-off early each morning, taking lunch with them and not returning until after dark. They reported the new yards were progressing steadily, however it would be another week or more before completion—even longer if the weather broke.

"Digging holes in the wet is fraught with problems."

John grinned as he scrubbed the mud from his arms and boots under the outside hose. "We're hoping to have the posts finished before that predicted cold front reaches us."

Having spent the past few months enjoying morning tea and lunch breaks with both John and his parents, Dawn's days had once again become long and lonely. She listlessly wandered around the house, straightening the lounge cushions, wiping a speck of dust off the record player, and staring at the tins in the pantry, filled to capacity with madeira cake, Anzac biscuits, and shortbread. One late autumn day, sick of her own company, she decided on the spur of the moment to visit Ed.

With renewed vigour, she packed an assortment of home cooking into smaller containers and tidied her hair. Collecting her gumboots and equipment bag first, she closed the back door behind her, and bent down to pick Poppy up as she brushed against her legs.

"You stay here and look after the house. I'll be back later." She lowered her to the ground next to the saucer of milk and hurried to the car.

Driving up Ed's lane toward the five-barred gate brought a sense of déjà vu, and a feeling of serenity settled into Dawn's bones. The soft foliage of the gardens and trees blended with the white-painted archway, inviting the visitor into the house yard. She parked her car by the gate, stepped out and smiled at the fantails, flitting above an ancient wheelbarrow overflowing with a rainbow of colourful flowers. A dog barked and she lifted her gaze to watch the big man stride toward her, a bird perched on his shoulder and the black and white collie at his heels.

"Hello." She waved and reached back into the car for the tin of baked goods. A sudden and unexpected shyness overcame her as she remembered how reclusive and private he could be. She had completely ignored the fact and now wished she had telephoned in advance.

"What a lovely surprise. Have you come to join me for a cup of tea?" Ed asked. A beam spread across his weather-beaten face and his deep blue eyes sparkled.

"Yes. If that's alright?" Still hesitant, she stood her ground for a few moments before he beamed and threw open the gate.

"Please. Come inside."

She followed him to the front door and slipped off her shoes.

"I apologise if I smell of smoke. I went fishing yesterday and have mullet to hang in the smokehouse."

She laughed and followed Ed down the hallway. "Ooh, lovely. I have grown to rather enjoy smoked mullet with parsley sauce. It's one of John's favourites and not something I grew up eating, so it's a good thing I like it."

He methodically boiled the kettle and spooned tea into the blue-patterned teapot while she watched on. After filling the pot with boiling water, he turned it twice one way and once the other, then poured the deep brown liquid into their cups. It was the exact same action she had witnessed her grandmother perform a million times over, and a nostalgic lump rose in her throat. She prised the lid off one of the containers she had brought, releasing the appetising scent of madeira cake. Reaching for the knife from Ed's hand, she cut slices and placed them on the plates.

"Did you drink tea in Norway?" She wasn't sure what prompted her, but suddenly, she was hungry for knowledge of his culture. The thought of him ending up on New Zealand's shores after a childhood in the frozen north triggered her interest. She wanted to know what foods he grew up eating and hear about the adjustments he had been forced to make over his lifetime.

"Of course. Perhaps a little different to how I like it now, but we always had a hot drink to begin and finish the day with." Silence filled the room while they both took a mouthful of cake.

"Very good." He waved his piece in the air and smiled.

Dawn relaxed against the wall, comfortable on the built-in seat with its thick wool-filled cushion and glanced out into the garden, her pulse quickening as she silently begged for more information. "Your vegetable garden is still very full. Are those potatoes ready for harvesting?"

He followed her gaze and nodded. "Yes, a few

more potatoes, then it will be turnips for the winter pot with plenty of cabbage and cauliflower. The Norwegian diet is very plain and I used to eat nothing but porridge, fish, turnips, and potatoes, but your mother-in-law—and the war—put an end to that." He chuckled softly and pointed to the row of jars on the side bench, filled with a amber-coloured liquid. "My bees have kindly provided me with honey for the next few months, so I'm a New Zealander now."

"Do you miss Norway?"

"No. I remember the happy times but I don't miss the cold … or the short, dark days of winter." He stopped and stared out of the window while a muscle in his jaw twitched. It was as though he needed to continue but didn't know how. Dawn ran her finger around the pattern on her saucer while she waited, praying that he would tell her more.

"My parents died when I was a teenager. I had an older sister, though, and I sometimes wonder what she is doing now."

Dawn sat bolt upright. A sister? That was amazing. She'd always wanted a sister herself. "Have you tried to contact her?"

She couldn't imagine having a loved sibling on the other side of the world and not trying to involve them in her life—it didn't seem reasonable. But … she acknowledged that, in spite of the difficult relationship she shared with her mother, she had at least experienced a secure home and a loving grandmother. *Perhaps they were two things Ed never had?*

He slid his chair back and walked across the room, withdrew a tiny address book from the pile of papers on the fridge, and returned, opening it before placing it on the table in front of her. She read the neat, loopy handwriting listed under the letter H.

Hilde Hansen, Ilsvikora 23, Trondheim, Norway

She stared at him before reading the note a second time. "Your sister?"

"Yes. It is the address of our childhood home. I don't know if it is still there but have wasted many years." He shrugged. "Perhaps she is no longer alive, or if she is, she no longer lives in the area. I could not continue my life without trying to contact her."

"So … you've written to her?"

"Yes." He shrugged again before continuing. "Five years ago with no reply. At least I have tried."

"Thank you for telling me." Dawn relaxed against the wall, lulled by a sense of companionship. On one hand, he was a stranger. On the other, by sharing this information it was as though he had included her in something that cemented a bond between the two of them.

With their cups now empty, Ed moved to the fridge and pulled out a saucer, holding it toward Dawn.

"Time to feed a hungry mouth." He smiled and led her to a cage beside the laundry tub. Sitting on a branch inside was a young swamp harrier, it's piercing gaze alertly glued to Dawn. The hawk still wore a fluffy coat of down with a few shiny feathers beginning to appear on its wings.

"I have been catching large insects and whatever small mammals I can find and also sharing tiny pieces of meat with him."

Dawn stood at a cautious distance as the sharply hooked beak gobbled the offering from Ed's tweezers and squawked for more.

"Would you like to learn how to feed the young birds I have?"

Dawn thought for a few seconds before answering. "Why not?"

She was fascinated by the injured and orphaned birds, and Ed's caring attitude resonated with her. She had months to wait for the baby to arrive—and anyway, even after the birth, learning more about nature was something she looked forward to. *I've got a lot of years to catch up on.*

After a tour of the aviary and a check of the feathered patients, she collected her hairdressing kit from the car, and quickly trimmed Ed's hair.

"It's time to bring the cows in for milking now. Would you like to come for a walk?"

"I'd love to." Dawn leapt to her feet, and they ambled up the lane to where the small herd of jersey cows waited patiently behind the neatly trimmed hedge. With a quick movement, Ed swung the gate open and the pretty, soulful-eyed bovines hurried through the opening and plodded toward the cowshed. As Ed and Dawn followed them, Ed answered the barrage of farming-related questions Dawn had been hesitant to ask either John or Harry for fear of making them have to repeat themselves too many times.

The afternoon sun was barely visible above the western horizon when she waved goodbye and drove steadily home. As she crawled past the house and drove into the garage, a warm comfort crept over her. With a shock, she realised that she no longer saw the house as poky or lacking character. It was hers and John's … and it was home.

CHAPTER 12

Pain hit her like a lightning strike—without warning or hesitation. She dropped to her knees. The firewood in her arms crashed to the floor. As she panted hard, the agony eased and she drew herself to her feet and crawled onto the couch. Another sharp ache began, peaked, and faded, and minutes later, a third had her staggering to the kitchen.

What's happening?

She was barely halfway through her pregnancy and was in excellent health, according to the doctor. An anxious glance at the clock told her it would be another hour or more before John came in for tea, and today of all days, Alice had decided to meet her sister in Auckland City for lunch and wouldn't return until late.

The pains dissipated and she breathed a sigh of relief, stoked the fire, and curled up under a blanket in front of its soothing warmth with a hot water bottle resting against her stomach. Hoping that John and Harry would return from the run-off earlier than usual, she was almost ashamed of her overwhelming relief when the rumble of the truck echoed in the half dark.

Voices carried in the still air, and a door slammed before the vehicle moved off again. John's tuneless whistle sounded in the back room as water splashed into the tub.

As though on cue, the pain began again, and by the time John strode down the hall calling for her, she was doubled up on the floor, barely able to speak.

He froze in the doorway before rushing to her side. "What's the matter? Are you sick?"

"I don't know. Terrible pain." Her voice was a mere whisper as John attempted to sit her up. "I think it's the baby."

"Oh, no. I've got to get you to hospital."

Vaguely aware of being carried to the car, Dawn lay immobile against John's chest. He smelled of sawdust, sweat, and the fresh scent of Sunlight Soap. With her head propped on a pillow and a wool blanket covering her, she was barely aware of the engine kicking into life. Her focus became little more than a fog of pain mixed with the jarring of her whole being as they struck potholes and the car roared into the night.

———

Lights burned her eyes, and she closed her lids tightly as her consciousness returned. She wrinkled her nose, the stench of disinfectant so strong, and her heart sank.

"I'm here, love. Right next to you." John's hand clutched hers, and he kissed her cheek gently.

"The baby?" Her voice rasped, unrecognisable as her own.

"I'm sorry, love. You've had a miscarriage." His tanned face had lost all colour and his chin trembled. "There was nothing the doctor could do to save the baby."

Numbness crept silently over her. Nothing. Voices disappeared into the distance and even the smell of disinfectant faded. She turned her head away, ignoring her husband's helpless gaze, and closed her eyes.

———

Returning to their little house was the hardest thing Dawn had done. She couldn't bear to look at the bassinet standing in the corner of the spare room, or the pile of baby wraps and gowns she had made, lovingly embroidering the yokes with tiny rosebuds and leaves exactly as her grandmother had taught her years before. Firmly shutting the door on them all, she shoved the huge bunch of flowers Susan and George had given her as John collected her from the hospital into a vase and wandered outside.

For the next few days she spent more time outside than ever, fiercely turning the soil in the vegetable garden, smashing clods of dirt, and raking the surface in readiness for more peas and broad beans. When rain threatened, she pulled on an oilskin coat and, taking Gyp with her, trudged across the home paddock and down the hill to the beach. She sat with her back against the grassy bank, oblivious to the cold, damp sand. The waves rolled gently toward her, lapping at her feet as though taunting her, vying for her attention before they gave up and receded. Seagulls screeched overhead and she stared at them blankly.

Almost a month after her miscarriage, she fiercely thumped the hoe into the dirt, chopping the lumps into fine particles so she could plant winter vegetables. Straightening her back, her gaze fixed on Alice's little grey car bouncing toward the house. Alice had called in every day, and if Dawn wasn't there, she left soup or a casserole on the kitchen bench. Her quiet manner was comforting and they talked about the weather, the garden, the latest news from John's brothers and Alice's sisters—anything except the subject of children.

"Is there anything I can do to help you, Dawn?" Alice's voice was firmer today. Purposeful. "Perhaps it's time for you to talk about it more."

Dawn shook her head as irritation began to prickle. She picked at an imaginary thread on her slacks. "I said no," Dawn replied, her cheeks heating. "You don't understand how I feel. The doctor said it will take time."

"Actually, I do know how you feel."

Dawn's head snapped up, meeting her mother-in-law's gentle but determined eyes.

Alice reached out and took her hand, holding it firmly as though sensing Dawn's urge to snatch it away. "I, too, lost a baby. In fact, I lost two."

Dawn stared at her, narrowing her eyes in doubt. *Are you just trying to make me feel better?*

"It's true. Before George was born, I had a miscarriage. Very similar to your situation, I was almost halfway through the pregnancy and thought all was well."

"Oh." A stab of shock threw her full attention on the woman sitting in front of her and she straightened, waiting for Alice to continue.

"That's not all. We also had a daughter. Emmeline. We called her Emmie and she was the apple of Harry's eye. Anyway, when she was three months old, whooping cough swept through the community and Emmie got a bad dose of it. She died and was buried in the church cemetery in Karaka."

"Oh," Dawn repeated. She didn't know what else to say and her heart melted. *Poor Alice. I've lost one baby but Alice lost two.* She stared at her mother-in-law, understanding the pain in her soft grey eyes and suddenly, something deep inside Dawn was released, as though a flood gate had been thrown open. Tears trickled down her cheeks and within a minute, the tide broke and she sobbed, noisily and unashamedly for the first time in years. Alice wrapped her arms around her, and the two of them remained as one for a long time. Eventually, Dawn stepped back and took the handkerchief from her mother-in-law, mopping her face and blowing her nose.

"I'll make us a cup of tea," Alice said.

In the quiet kitchen, the women sipped their hot drinks and stared through the window to the hills and valley below.

Returning her gaze to Dawn, Alice continued. "I know you probably think Harry and I have spoiled John. It's true that he has had more attention than the older boys, but he was our miracle, you see. After Emmie, the doctor told me I couldn't have any more children, so no one was more surprised than he when we realised I was pregnant again."

Dawn's eyes widened as understanding seeped into her. Guilt and shame clouded her emotions. She had not appreciated the kindness that both Harry and Alice had shown her—she'd even thought they were selfish and controlling, perhaps at times deliberately trying to keep John from her. She had got it all wrong.

Her lip quivered as tears threatened again.

"I'd better get home now. The cow needs to be brought in and the chooks fed." Alice folded her hand over Dawn's again and gave her a gentle smile. "Are you alright, dear?"

Dawn nodded and drew a deep breath before standing to hug Alice. "I am. Thank you for sharing your stories with me."

"Well …" Alice removed her jacket from the back of the chair. "I know how sad you're feeling, but you're not alone. Please never feel that you can't talk to me about anything. I promise you, I will never judge you—and I do understand." She reached out and squeezed Dawn's arm. "It's been a while since we had a stroll through the bush and visited the fantails. Next time you're near our place, let's do it again."

Dawn twisted her mouth as a picture of the cool bush track with its thick foliage of ferns and trees sprang to her memory. Then, for the first time in what felt like an age, she smiled.

As though Mother Nature also understood, the clouds cleared and the late autumn sun glistened on the puddles as the two women walked to the car. Birds chirped and chattered, fighting over worms and insects that hovered on the damp ground.

She waved a fond farewell, waiting until the little car disappeared from sight before returning to the kitchen with a lightness to her step.

———

THAT EVENING, SHE AND JOHN DEMOLISHED THE shepherd's pie and lemon delicious pudding Dawn made before sitting together in front of the fire. Songs from the Bee Gees emanated from the record player in the corner and Dawn leaned against her husband, pressing her body into his as though needing them to meld into one.

John held her tight, stroking her hair and staring into the flames.

She felt the tension slide from his body as she spoke. "I love you more than I could ever imagine."

He held her face between his hands and whispered, "And I love you too. We have each other, and that is enough."

She nodded, a warmth creeping through her as he slid the guard in front of the fire and reached for her hand.

"It's bedtime."

CHAPTER 13

Throughout the winter, Dawn's visits to Ed had become one of the highlights of her week. While her knowledge and interest increased with the injured and dependent birds and animals, her driving confidence also received a boost. And, as the bond between her and the elderly man strengthened, she found a voice she didn't know she had and shared snippets from her childhood.

He would nod, occasionally asking her to elaborate as she shared stories of her grandmother's baking and her mother's strict lessons, but mostly he listened in silence, his lack of interference encouraging her further. She stopped to wonder about her father and the little she knew about him. What might life have been like had he lived? If he were here now, would they share a similar bond to the one she was developing with Ed?

"Perhaps I was a mistake? An unwanted baby?" She stared at Ed, and he shook his head.

"Perhaps it was none of those things. One day, you will find the right time to talk to your mother." He gave her a small smile as she packed her empty baking container in the car, glancing up as a bicycle came wobbling up his lane.

Dawn's eyes widened as she swung her gaze between Ed and the cyclist. "It's Carol."

"Yes, it is. She visits periodically, although not as often as you do. Has a way with the animals." His words were clipped, and Dawn frowned as the woman drew closer.

"Hello Dawn." Carol leaned the bike against the fence and wound the scarf around her neck a little more snuggly.

"Hello again. How lovely to see you." Dawn's smile faded as she caught sight of a large purple bruise rising up Carol's throat and onto her jawline. "Have you hurt yourself?"

Carol turned her collar up and shrunk into her jacket. "Oh, it's nothing. I slipped in the cowshed and fell." She turned to face Ed, dismissing Dawn's questioning gaze. "I've come to see how the patients are doing today."

While she and Carol fed the pigs, Dawn slid her gaze sideways and studied the pale-faced woman. Her strength seemed to defy her thin body as she heaved the buckets of milk and poured it into the troughs while Dawn struggled to keep up with her. Her fine blonde hair hung in rats' tails, straggling over her shoulders, and Dawn longed to take her scissors to it.

Carol glanced up and met her eyes. "Ed says you're a hairdresser and his regular barber now." She placed the empty buckets at her feet and raised her hands to her head. "I—I was wondering if you would be able to trim my hair for me some time."

Guilt flooded through Dawn. *She read my mind.* "I would love to. Would you like to come to my house … or should I go to yours?"

"No, no." She shook her head violently. "If I know when you're coming next, we can meet here. Ed won't mind."

Dawn hesitated and attempted to hide her surprise. "Of course. That's no trouble. I always carry my hairdressing kit in the car anyway, so I could do it as soon as we finish here?"

Carol's hand flew to her throat and she shook her head. "No, not today. Perhaps next Wednesday." Then she picked up the buckets and turned away, hurrying to catch Ed as he headed toward the bird aviary.

Dawn narrowed her eyes as she followed the slight woman across the paddock. Uneasiness wormed its way inside her. She suddenly felt like an outsider, excluded from whatever it was that Carol and Ed shared. She scrubbed the buckets and turned them upside down.

"Sorry, Ed. I promised Alice I'd be home early today so I can give her a hand."

If Ed was surprised, he didn't show it, and Dawn waved a hasty goodbye to the two silent figures and climbed gratefully into her car.

———

A PHEASANT RAN ACROSS THE ROAD IN FRONT OF HER, and Dawn slammed on the brakes.

"Phew. That was close." She breathed out, changed down a gear, and forced her concentration on the road ahead. As she approached their driveway, she slowed, her mind in free fall, and on the spur of the moment, she drove straight past, continuing down the hill to the homestead.

Finding Alice at the clothesline, Dawn helped her collect and fold the sheets and towels while they chatted. In the winter chill, darkness was approaching rapidly, and Dawn studied the older woman's kind face—her fair complexion, surrounded by the neat cloud of snow-white hair as clear and healthy as her eyes. She had a vibrance about her and a quick humour that even the most negative temperament couldn't resist.

"Alice, do you know a woman named Carol? I met her at the New Year's Eve dance. Thin and blonde haired," she asked.

Alice looked up slowly, her gaze steady. "Why do you ask?"

Dawn fiddled with the pillowcases on the pile and twisted her lips. "She came to Ed's today while I was there. It seems she visits him regularly too—on her bicycle."

"Well, their farm is only a couple of miles away, so that wouldn't be a struggle. She married Ronald a couple of years ago but I don't really know her. She doesn't come to any of the community events, as a rule. In fact, I think the dance would be the first time I've seen her for over a year. She came to a couple of church services after their wedding but ..." A frown formed on Alice's face.

"Oh, I didn't realise she had a husband. Was he at the dance? She seemed to be with an elderly couple."

"I didn't see him." Alice flicked the tea towel she was folding so hard it gave a snap in the air. "He would have been out the back drinking, I imagine. I didn't recognise the people she was with either. Perhaps they were some relation or other staying for Christmas and New Year?"

"D-do you think it's a happy marriage?"

"I have no idea, love." She stood still and met Dawn's eyes. "It's probably best we mind our own business and don't get involved."

Heat crept up Dawn's neck and she nodded silently. *Hmm. Perhaps if Carol lets me cut her hair we can become friends. I think she needs one.*

A lump of apprehension sat deep in the pit of her stomach as she made her way up the hill to their cottage. *It must have been a strange fall to have caused that bruise on Carol's neck.*

———

THE FOLLOWING WEEK BROUGHT HEAVY RAIN AND GALE-force winds, and Dawn was not surprised when Carol didn't turn up at Ed's the following Wednesday.

"Do you think I should go and collect her?"

"No." Ed's stern tone surprised her. He paused for a few seconds before continuing, more gently this time. "Stay well away from that place. Carol's life is different to yours, and you would not be helping her."

"Oh." Dawn was lost for words. *Is Carol in some kind of trouble that Ed knows about?* She bent over the bird cage that a neighbour had dropped into Ed's, driving out the gate as Dawn waited to turn in. It contained a terrified Kereru and she studied its glossy green feathers before facing Ed again. "Are we able to splint this bird's leg?"

His face softened and he reached into the cage, encasing the entire bird in his huge hand. Gently stroking the broken leg, he frowned. "We'll have to. It looks like a clean break so we'll make a splint as small as possible to keep the joint above it mobile and give him a few days of cage rest while it knits. Our biggest worry is stress. You've seen what that does."

Dawn frowned. That had been the most difficult

lesson over the past few months. It didn't seem to matter how much care, warmth, food, and love she showered on the patients—some died anyway, and it was only John's regular kind words that kept her going. *"If it wasn't for what you and Ed are doing, they would all be dead anyway. At least you try—and that's all you can do. Nature can be fickle."*

How true. The months came and went and the pain of losing the baby eased, but never died. The strength and kindness Alice showed boosted Dawn on, together with the hope that another pregnancy would happen soon.

She concentrated on the job at hand, holding the bird firmly while Ed tended to the broken leg. It was the final chore for the day with the exception of the late afternoon milking, and Dawn was looking forward to their usual cup of tea and friendly chat before she headed home. Guilt at her rapid departure the previous week left her wanting to make amends.

With the Kereru safely bandaged and comfortable, Ed boiled the kettle and they enjoyed a hot drink in front of the lounge fire. Although now used to Ed's reserved manner, today, Dawn's concern grew. She had never seen him quite this distracted—quiet, reclusive, and thoughtful, yes—but brooding and silent was completely out of the ordinary. *Something is troubling him—and whatever it is, it's not good.*

The afternoon was closing in with dark clouds building when Ed gathered their cups.

She followed him to the kitchen and picked up her coat. "Shall I help you bring the cows in?"

"Thank you, but no. It's going to rain soon, and I'd rather you got home safely."

She nodded and headed toward the door. "See you next week?"

"Of course." He smiled and her anxiety eased a little. "I look forward to it."

———

SHE TRUNDLED UP AND DOWN THE HILLS AND PUTTERED carefully around the sharp corners, forcing her thoughts from Ed to tonight's tea. John and Harry had been planning to shift a mob of cattle to the run-off, and a day of mustering on horseback would generate a healthy appetite. If she turned the oven on the minute she walked in the door, there would be time to roast a tray of vegetables to go with the lamb chops, and she would make an apple sponge pudding for dessert. Feeling pleased with herself, she sang heartily as she rounded the last bend and turned into their home paddock.

Her disappointment was fleeting when she opened the empty flour bin and remembered she had used the last of it to make the shortbread she'd taken to Ed's.

Oh well. Looks like a day in town tomorrow for me. She cheerfully stewed the apples with a few stalks of rhubarb and set to making a pot of custard instead.

———

INSTEAD OF HEADING STRAIGHT INTO TOWN THE following morning, she turned off only a mile or so beforehand and followed the main road towards Auckland. A minute later, she pulled into the wide driveway that led to the red-timbered home where Jill and Tim lived. The small paddock in front of the house held half a dozen sheep and was edged with several rows of pine trees. Tim's latest sideline was apparently selling Christmas trees.

Two little boys raced up and down the veranda on their bikes, leaping off them as she stopped outside the back gate.

Jill threw open the back door, the youngest child on her hip, and brushed the hair from her face. Her smile widened, and she wrapped her spare arm around Dawn.

"It's so good to see you again. Come in. The kettle has just boiled."

Dawn glanced around the room. A spinning wheel stood in one corner, surrounded by baskets of wool of every shade and stage. Some tightly wound balls vied for space amongst a set of wooden blocks, and a toy truck lay on the floor with a trailer full of unspun wool attached to it. Clean washing overflowed from its basket onto the couch, the kitchen bench was covered with bits of paper, half-eaten sandwiches, and a bowl of fruit, while a large pot bubbled on the stove, emitting a tantalising smell of citrus and sticky sweetness.

"I'm in the middle of making marmalade. A friend brought me a box of grapefruit and lemons and they needed using before they go off." Jill shrugged apologetically, and Dawn reached for the toddler.

"Let me take Richard for you." She smiled and hoisted him onto her hip with both arms. "Goodness, you're getting so big." She shot Jill a glance. "How do you do it?"

Jill grimaced and waved her hand around the room. "With great difficulty, as you can see." She laughed helplessly then, and Dawn joined in, relaxing under Jill's easy-going welcome.

Her own house was small, immaculate, and the complete opposite to the shambles she now stood in. However, this home oozed warmth, happiness, and a love that filled her soul.

"Excuse the mess. Poor Alice has fifty fits when she visits, but I've never been very organised. Having a tidy house is not a priority for me. Sometimes I feel a bit guilty, but I can't help myself." Jill shrugged apologetically and Dawn smiled.

"It's not everything. I would much rather exchange my orderly home for one that's untidy but includes a child." She bit her lip, surprised at her admission. *I don't share my feelings with anyone.*

Jill turned the stove off. "Put that great lump of a

child down. Have you got time to help me bottle this jam?"

For the next hour, the young women chatted about family, gardening, and recipes. Dawn let her guard down for the first time in a long time, sharing her fears and problems with Jill. While her sister-in-law ladled jam into the array of clean jars, wiped them clean, and labelled them, Dawn did her best to tidy the kitchen and intermittently occupy the children. Matchbox vehicles of every shape and colour were spread across a rug on the floor and a toy garage, complete with a hoist and ramps, seemed to amuse the boys the most. Dawn was grateful that her role appeared to be simply having to select the next vehicle to be 'fixed' and nothing more.

"I think there's a strong suggestion here that these little fellows follow their dad's example?" Dawn grinned at Jill as they sipped a cup of tea.

"There sure is. Alice said Tim used to drive Harry mad, pulling everything apart and rebuilding it when he was young—and he certainly encourages the boys to do the same."

Half an hour later Dawn reluctantly reached for the empty cups and placed them in the sink. She gave the children a cuddle and turned back to Jill.

"Why don't you all come out to the farm next weekend? We're going out to the run-off to see how the marram grass and lupins are going. John reckons the first flowers should be opening by now. The jonquils and daffodils in my garden are about to bloom too," Dawn said.

"That sounds lovely. We'll bring a picnic and the boys can run wild," Jill called.

Dawn laughed again and waved goodbye. Driving away from the house, she chuckled. The boys running wild was something she could picture very clearly.

CHAPTER 14

Dawn finished loading her groceries in the boot, moving the package containing a new shirt and Harper Lee's book, *To Kill a Mockingbird* that she'd bought for John. As an avid reader—apparently encouraged from an early age by Paddy, the old Irishman—it had been difficult to find a title that John hadn't read, and Dawn was looking forward to seeing his reaction when he opened the present on their wedding anniversary this coming weekend.

As Dawn drove up the main street, a soft, white bunny-rug caught her eye in the Draper's window and she pulled into the kerb and parked. *Perfect for Ann's new baby.* With the blanket carefully wrapped in tissue paper and resting on top of the shirt and book, Dawn glanced in the rear-view mirror and pulled out onto the road facing home.

Oh cripes! I nearly forgot the parcel John asked me to collect.

She did a U-turn and headed to the train station where a box of farm books from George was waiting. According to George, his parcel was too expensive to send via post and would need to be transported by train.

Parking as close as she could to the freight office, Dawn got out and opened the gate leading to the platform. A tall, elderly woman stood outside the building, and Dawn shot her a smile as she passed. Grateful for the young porter's assistance, she hurried to open the boot door and stood back, allowing the man to place the heavy parcel next to the groceries. Thanking him, she returned to the driver's seat before glancing again at the woman. Having moved a few steps closer to the gate, the lady seemed to be waiting for someone or something. A familiarity about her disturbed Dawn and she wrinkled her brow as she searched the depths of her memory. The porter had disappeared and with no one in sight, Dawn opened her door and stepped out again.

"Are you waiting for someone? Can I help at all?"

The woman's face wore a stern, creased expression, as though filled with a dozen worries. Her long, dark coat covered a tall, thin frame, and her cloche hat reminded Dawn of her own grandmother. "I—I do not know."

"You don't know … if someone is coming to meet you?"

The woman twisted her gloved hands together and glanced down at the small leather suitcase at her feet. "No. Yes." She shook her head and Dawn was afraid she was about to cry. "I don't know what to do." Her voice was deep and heavily accented—although Dawn couldn't recognise where the accent was from.

Dawn glanced around. Should she offer to take her to the hospital—or perhaps the police station? She held her hand out. "My name is Dawn Simpson."

The woman took it gently and nodded. "I am Hilde Hansen."

Dawn almost choked as she stared into the deep blue eyes and noted the strong bone structure of the woman's jaw. "Ed's sister?"

The older woman's eyes widened and deep creases formed on her forehead. "Ed? I have a brother. Edvard. He lives at South Head. I ask if a bus can take me but no. No bus. No train. No car."

Dawn clutched the front of her collar as her mind raced. Was this Ed's sister? He hadn't mentioned anything about Hilde's visit yesterday. But then, he hadn't received a reply to his letter—and it had been five years!

"I know Ed. In fact, I was at his house only yesterday. Would you like to come with me? I can take you to him."

Relief flooded the woman's face, and she stepped

back and leaned briefly against the building. Dawn thought she might collapse and lurched forward, and extended a hand. Instead of taking it, the woman bent and picked up her suitcase before straightening her shoulders and meeting Dawn's startled eyes.

"Please. That would be very nice."

Dawn stood still for a few seconds before ushering the woman to her car. After stowing the suitcase on the back seat next to the parcel, Dawn gestured for Hilde to get into the front passenger seat and closed the door.

She started the engine and reversed out, then waited at the kerb for a minute. "I need to make a phone call before we set off. It's quite a long drive, and my husband will worry if I am away too long."

Guilt flickered within her at the lie. John knew she was in town today and wouldn't worry at all. Nevertheless, she thought some warning might be necessary in the circumstances.

Hilde nodded and gripped the bag on her lap more firmly.

"I'll be two minutes." Dawn removed the key from the ignition, dithering over whether she should be leaving her, even if only for a short period. She grabbed her purse and darted into the telephone booth outside the post office.

Ed's phone rang out, and she asked the operator to try another number. This time, Alice's cheerful voice answered, and Dawn breathed a sigh of relief.

"Oh, thank goodness you're there, Alice." She hastily

told her about the unexpected encounter with Ed's sister and waited for Alice's response.

"Really? My goodness … well, you'd better bring her here first. While you're driving, we'll see if we can get on to Ed and give him some notice. I suspect this will be quite a shock—and who knows if it will be a good one or bad?"

"Thanks Alice. See you within the hour." She hung up and hurried back to the car.

Hilde hadn't moved, her gloved fingers still clutching the bag on her lap. Only her eyes darted left and right while her thin lips remained closed.

"You poor thing. You must be very tired. How far have you come today? When did you arrive in New Zealand?" Dawn's bombardment of questions seemed to confuse the woman even further, and she stared through the windscreen in silence.

"I'm sorry. I didn't mean to pry." Dawn spoke more slowly this time and focused on driving. They passed through Parakai, crossed the flats, and were winding their way around the third headland before Hilde said a word.

"I come by boat. A long journey, and I learn English … not very well."

"Don't worry about that," Dawn said. She smiled and continued, "I think it's wonderful that you have come at all. Ed will be surprised but happy. He is well respected here."

"Respected? Please?"

"Liked. Everyone likes him. He helps us. He has been a good friend of my husband's family for a long, long time."

Hilde's face softened, the hint of a smile tipping her lips. She stared out of the window, bobbing her head occasionally. Dawn wasn't sure if it meant she approved of her surroundings—or was trying to stay awake?

Their arrival at Fantail Ridge was greeted by Alice, Harry, and John, and while Alice ushered Hilde inside and directed her to the bathroom, John hugged Dawn and whispered in her ear, "I'm pleased you went to town today. Imagine what the poor woman might have done if you hadn't come along."

"I know. She's worried her English isn't very good, and she doesn't know anybody here. I think the sooner we can reunite her with Ed, the better."

Harry made a pot of tea while Dawn opened the tin and cut slices of apple tea cake.

"Hmm. Ed is still not answering his phone. Probably busy milking, so Mum thinks Hilde should stay here until after tea and then we can deliver her to Ed's," John said.

Dawn didn't have time to answer before both Alice and Hilde returned to the living room.

Her eyes darted from one to the other as the Norwegian woman seemed to struggle to follow the conversation around the table. She asked why Ed hadn't come to collect her, and it took Alice several attempts to explain that he didn't know about her arrival. Eventually, Hilde appeared to relax, smiling when it seemed she realised the invitation to stay for a meal was genuine. "Then we go. See my brother."

"Yes." Alice touched her arm. "Now, you must stay. You eat with us and then we will take you to Edvard's home."

Hilde's smile widened and the signs of strain and exhaustion mellowed as her face became calm.

———

WHILE ALICE AND HARRY ENCOURAGED HILDE TO REST, Dawn and Harry hurried home to unpack the car and feed the animals earlier than usual in order to return to the homestead for tea. While John tended to the dogs and chooks, Dawn slid a bacon and egg pie and a cake into the oven.

Reappearing in the kitchen, John enveloped her in a hug and rasped his unshaven jaw against her cheek. "Something smells good."

She laughed and swatted him away, her hands resting on his shoulders as she spoke. "I got hold of Ed and he's in shock, but in a nice way I think. He's excited too and didn't want to talk long because he 'needed to prepare his home'." She chuckled. "I also thought if we are all going to descend on Ed this evening, especially delivering his long, lost sister, the least I could do is to arrive with enough food to keep he and Hilde going for a meal or two. You know Ed only goes to town once a month and lives on the basics anyway. I'm not sure what Hilde is used to eating, but there's not much meat on her bones so whatever it is, she needs more."

"You're a thoughtful woman. No wonder I love you so much." John hugged her again and they kissed.

"Gosh, I just thought—this will be the first time since he was shipwrecked forty-five years ago that he will have had anyone else under his roof except him."

She raised her eyebrows as John's words sank in. "I wonder how he'll feel about that."

"I'll duck through the shower." John paused in the doorway. "How about I collect a bit of mutton from the freezer to take out as well. I know Ed has plenty of fish, but you know how much he enjoys a bit of lamb."

She grinned and extracted the pie. "You'd better get a wriggle on. Your mother will have a beautiful evening meal ready soon and something tells me she won't want to wait."

———

A TEAR TRICKLED DOWN ED'S FACE AS HILDE STOOD IN front of him, and Dawn choked back the lump in her throat. Surrounded by the Simpson family, the two Norwegians stood almost a head taller than any of them, and Dawn blinked. At five-foot-nine-inches, she had spent her life being the tallest in her class, the tallest in the salon, and was used to being eye to eye with her husband. Beside the Hansen's, she felt small and insignificant.

Ed brushed a sleeve over his face and indicated for them to enter his house. Dawn and Alice hovered in the tiny kitchen, unpacking the food they had brought and laying it on the table, while Harry and John stood side by side in the doorway. Ed ushered his sister into the spare room as the word *"tak"* was repeated again and again by Hilde.

"Thank you," whispered Dawn. She glanced around the room. It was always spotless but this evening, everything seemed to have an extra shine on it. She glanced at her reflection in the kettle, her face distorted by its concave shape, and smiled at her round cheeks and freckled nose.

It took several minutes before everyone sat down, squashed into the room, and seated on a variety of stools, chairs, and even a step ladder.

"Thank you for bringing my sister to me. It is the nicest surprise I have had in many years." Ed stumbled over the words, coughing, his voice shaky.

He looked at Hilde again and she smiled in return, speaking a few words in Norwegian. He frowned slightly and answered in his native tongue before apologising to the Simpsons.

"I am sorry. I have asked Hilde to speak only English when we have visitors. She does not understand that it is rude to speak Norwegian in company. We will use it when alone."

Alice waved her hand and smiled sympathetically at Hilde. "She has only just arrived in this country, Ed. I'm sure it won't bother any of us if we can't understand her. Perhaps we will have more opportunity to learn your language now." Ed inclined his head and solemnly gave a small nod as Alice got to her feet. "Anyway, I think it's time we left you two to catch up. I've no doubt you have a lot to talk about, and Hilde will be interested in having a look around."

Ed clasped Harry's hand before kissing Alice on both cheeks.

"I can never thank you all enough. You especially, Dawn." He turned to her and almost swallowed her in a bear hug. "I have felt a little strange lately—as if perhaps deep inside, I knew something was going to happen. I wasn't sure though if it was a good thing or bad."

Grinning, Dawn extracted herself and gave him a peck on the cheek. "It was meant to be, Ed. If I hadn't used the last of my flour on your shortbread yesterday, I would never have seen Hilde—so there you are. All's well that ends well."

A warm, satisfied glow seeped through her as they drove back to Fantail Ridge. She turned her head to gaze through the window. *How about that? You never know what is just around the corner.*

CHAPTER 15

From inside the cab, Alice once more peered through the small back window at the other passengers seated in the truck's rear tray. With their backs against a row of hay bales, Dawn, Tim, and Jill clung tightly to the three giggling children as the truck jolted through potholes and shuddered over bumps. To reassure everyone that all was well outside the safety of the cab, Alice gave the window a cheery tap.

Wispy clouds drifted slowly against the blue sky, and every now and then, a gust of wind blew over the ridge, rustling the leaves of the randomly scattered trees as they passed.

"We couldn't have picked a nicer day," Jill said. She had to raise her voice above the roar of the engine to be heard and Dawn smiled, nodding in agreement.

"I haven't been out here all winter," she said.

"And I haven't been out since the block was

purchased, so it's all new to me." Tim tucked Mark against Jill and got to his feet as the vehicle came to a halt in front of a wide timber gate. "I've got it."

He leapt off the truck tray and had the latch undone before Harry had time to swing his legs out of the open passenger door.

"Righto. Kids inside now as the track gets a bit rough." Harry reached up to take Richard from Jill, transferring him onto Alice's lap before helping both Mark and Jack into the cab. He slammed the door shut and climbed aboard the tray-back beside Dawn.

Facing forward and able to view the route ahead, the four adults stood hanging onto the frame behind the cab. Winding its way along the ridge, the truck descended to the wide, flat area of grassland that encompassed the new spiderweb of cattle yards. Minutes later, John braked and killed the ignition.

"We're here!" Harry announced before taking the lead and swinging himself off the side of the tray and onto the ground as if he were Dawn's age again. Once everyone had tumbled out of the truck, they followed John away from the yards and scrambled up the rise to the west, pausing on the summit.

"There it is. This is where Dad and I have been working for the best part of a year." John reached out and grabbed Dawn's hand, hauling her up the final peak to stand beside him.

Her jaw dropped as she gazed at the vista in front of her. New fences crisscrossed the bright green spring grasses, and rich, red Hereford cattle paused, lifted their heads to study the invasion, and returned to grazing. Beyond the cattle, the strip of sand dunes glowed grey-green, the wiry marram grass Dawn had helped plant earlier in the year rippling like the ocean in a breeze. Dotted amongst it in a thick swathe between the cattle and the sand, a palette of lemon, blue, pink, and mauve lupins stood tall and strong, providing a sea of glorious colour.

Dawn clapped her hands together and held them to her lips. "Aren't they gorgeous?"

She turned slightly as Jill came up beside her, breathless, and clutched her arm.

"Wow. You're not wrong. They're stunning," Jill puffed.

"Well, they're not in full bloom yet, so wait another few weeks and then you really will be amazed," John said.

"I had no idea that something supposedly so helpful with nutrients and all that stuff could look this good." Something inside Dawn blossomed, and her eyes misted. *I am part of this.* A sense of ownership, of creation and of belonging, filled her.

"Come on, everyone. Time for our picnic." Jill held Richard's hand while the older boys ran down the hill, their arms spread wide.

Dodging the moist cow pats scattered around the shaded areas of the paddock, the family selected a lush, grassy patch to lay out rugs and unpack the food. The air was still in the lea of the ridge and the early spring sun beat down, demanding jackets and thick jerseys be discarded.

A container of sandwiches was quickly consumed before Jill removed the lid from a large tin and carefully lifted out a sponge cake filled with strawberry jam and whipped cream. On the top of the pale golden creation, the words *Happy Anniversary* were piped in white icing.

"I know it's not until tomorrow, but it's not every day that we get together—and your first year of marriage and living on Fantail Ridge is worth celebrating." Jill leaned forward and kissed both Dawn and John on the cheek.

Flabbergasted by Jill's thoughtfulness, Dawn struggled to respond. "Th-thank you, Jill. You're so considerate."

With the excitement of Hilde's arrival and the distraction of the family outing to the run-off, she had almost forgotten that it was their wedding anniversary weekend.

Jill's cake was delicious and her kindness remained with Dawn for the rest of the excursion. Having no siblings had its disadvantages—and making celebration cakes for those close to you was not something either she or her mother had bothered with following the death of her grandmother. She reflected on Alice's meals and the pile of *Women's Weekly* magazines Jill had asked Alice to deliver to them after the miscarriage, and guilt surged inside her. *I haven't been a very good sister-in-law.* She took a deep breath and straightened her shoulders. *I will change that.*

They cleared the remnants of the picnic and picked up their jackets before climbing back onto the truck for a drive around the property. The truck bounced and stalled as John accelerated to climb a steep pinch, and he let the vehicle roll back down the rise.

"Everybody out! I'll have to drive around the long way. I'll take Mum and Richard with me and meet you all on the other side of the hill," John said.

"Come on, boys. Let's race to the top." Dawn grabbed Jack's hand as Mark took off up the slope. Once again, on reaching the crest, the scene in front of her halted Dawn, and she bent to catch her breath while the boys waved and shrieked at their parents and grandfather, struggling up the rise. A breeze swept in off the sea, encouraging the lupins to dance and bend under its strength. Something shifted inside Dawn. She couldn't remember seeing anything more beautiful in her whole life.

Her attention returned to the family around her and she smiled. It hadn't been an easy year, with more bumps in the road than she had expected. These people were kind, welcoming and supportive. She had resisted, and at times her impulsive and outspoken behaviour had obviously shocked those who cared about her most. But this was now her life and her family. It was time she grew up.

She tied her scarf under her chin, reached out to grasp a small hand in each of hers, and with a child on either side, she raced toward the lupins.

———

THAT NIGHT, SHE DIALLED SUSAN AND GEORGE'S number and waited while butterflies romped inside her.

"Hello? Susan's voice seemed to smile at the other end of the phone and the fluttering in Dawn's stomach immediately settled.

"Hello Susan. It's me, Dawn."

"How lovely to hear from you." Susan began brightly, then her voice softened. "Is everything alright?"

"Yes. It's fine. I know toll calls are expensive, but I'm not much of a letter writer and I wanted to say hello and thank you again for the flowers you gave me. They were gorgeous."

"Oh, Dawn. It was our pleasure, and I'm so sorry you had to go through such a horrid time. It's lovely to hear your voice."

With her eye on the clock, Dawn mellowed as their conversation switched from the children to the farm, to the animals and the goings on in South Head. Conscious of the high cost of long-distance calls, Dawn promised to ring again soon, and finished the chat. Her heart sang. She had never been good at making friends and having Ann living in the next street had made it easy to avoid trying. Now, she had actually taken the first step to bridging the gap between her and the other family members—and she let out a deep sigh of happiness.

CHAPTER 16

Spring 1971, Four years later

"I'm selling the house."

Dawn froze, perched on the edge of the telephone stool. What did her mother mean? They had lived in the same home all Dawn's life and after her grandmother's death, her mother had inherited it. So … she had a lovely home, albeit rather big for one person—and when Dawn thought about it, it probably was a lot of work. But nevertheless, it was her mother's.

"But why? You have someone do the garden and lawns, and it can't be too hard to clean with just you there?" Dawn asked.

"That's just it. It is too hard for me to manage now. It's old and shabby, and I don't have the money to maintain it. Mrs Bailey stopped coming months ago, and I can't afford to pay Mr Freeman anymore."

This revelation of financial stress was a shock.

Could it be true? Dawn opened and shut her mouth—like a fish without a sound. Having her mother confide in her compounded the surprise. She frowned into the phone as Lillian continued.

"I don't do as much sewing these days. There's such a variety available in the shops now, and many of my old customers have died or prefer to buy ready-made. So … most of the time, my widow's pension is all I have, and that's not exactly generous." Seconds of silence passed as Dawn digested this information.

"What do you want to do, Mum? Are you coming to live with us?" Dread filled Dawn as she considered this option. After the first Christmas on Fantail Ridge, Lillian had only returned once—when her bridge friends were away with their own families, and her choices were to stay at home alone or join her daughter and son-in-law for a few days on the farm. It had been a long, difficult visit.

"Absolutely not. I will not leave the city, or my area, for that matter. No, there's a nice block of units being built in the next street, and I have decided that the one facing the road will do me nicely. They're brick, low-maintenance, and very smart. I don't need a big place—just a bedroom for me and one for my sewing—with room for a bed in case you ever have to stay, of course."

Dawn twisted her lips in a wry grin. When did they ever stay in the city? On the one occasion she had visited the gynaecologist, George and Susan's gracious guest suite was more suitable, especially now that she and Susan had become firm friends—and it was walking distance to the doctor's office.

"Are you listening?" her mother snapped in her ear, and Dawn drew a deep breath.

"Yes, Mum. Of course I am. It's a bit of a surprise—that's all. So, when are you going to sell the house?"

"Actually, it's already under contract. I have signed the documents for the unit and will be moving there next month."

Dawn blinked hard and glanced at the calendar behind the kitchen door.

"So, if there's anything you'd like from the house, perhaps you and John could come and collect it as soon as possible or else I'll have to dispose of it." It wasn't a question—it was an ultimatum, and Dawn reeled at the haste with which her mother had operated. She delved into her memory. Had Lillian mentioned anything about downsizing during their weekly phone calls? She couldn't recollect—but then, she often switched off and let her mind wander while her mother rattled on. Guilt wormed its way through her as her mother's silence registered. "I see. Thank you. Yes, I will give it some thought and let you know when I ring on Sunday night. Is that enough time?"

"I suppose so. I have instructed the agent to sell whatever furniture in the house that the new buyer wants, with the exception of a few labelled items such as my bedroom suite and sewing desk. Oh, and your old bed, of course."

Visions of her grandmother's beautiful handmade timber furniture flooded her mind. She had so many memories of the chunky china cabinet and sideboard, complete with the dent and water mark where Dawn had accidently knocked a heavy crystal vase over as a child and it had broken. She could still feel her mother's hard slap on the back of her legs. A sudden picture of an old treasure flashed before her.

"Mum, do you use Gran's little writing desk? The one from her bedroom with the green leather top?"

"Not really. I did store papers in it after she died but I don't need it. I'll throw out the contents and you can have it if you want it. I will have considerably more money after the sale and intend buying some of that nice new slimline lounge furniture and a small, elegant table that will seat my bridge group nicely."

And that was that. The conversation ended swiftly and Dawn remained sitting on the stool for several minutes before she rose to prepare bottles of milk for the two orphan lambs she had in the pen beside the chooks.

The second they saw her they ran, bunting her legs and desperately seeking the teats. She laughed and bent down, holding the bottles tightly as they sucked ferociously, their tails wagging while gorging themselves on the warm milk. With the bottles empty, her thoughts returned to her mother and the startling news of her move. Gyp pressed against her legs.

"Well, Gyp. What do you think of that?" She rubbed

the dog's ears gently. "My old home will soon belong to someone else." The old gripe of guilt clenched her stomach. Memories of collecting fallen apples from the tree in the back garden, hiding behind the shed so her mother wouldn't see her eating them and accuse her of being greedy, suddenly returned. She sighed. "I hope the next family enjoy them more than I was allowed to. Are you coming over to the dairy with me?"

Gyp looked up at her with her soulful brown eyes and fell in step by her side. Dawn had to walk slowly initially until the old dog's joints freed up and they could increase the pace.

"Hi Charlie!" She yelled over the noise of the milking machines, and he waved in acknowledgement as he moved along the concrete herringbone pit to the next cow.

She tied Gyp up outside the shed before resting the milk billy on the shelf above the vat and fastened the plastic apron around her waist. For almost four years now she had been coming to help with the calves, forming a routine with Bev, who did the morning feeds as soon as her children got on the school bus, and Dawn doing the late afternoon feed. In spite of a second miscarriage in 1968, no further pregnancy had eventuated for Dawn and John, and Dawn had reluctantly resigned herself to a childless marriage. The bellowing, gambolling black and white calves filled a gap in her life, and she could barely remember the incompetent, needy young woman who had arrived on Fantail Ridge five years before.

She stood the large buckets in a row and measured milk powder into each one. Then, after adding warm water, she stirred the mixture thoroughly and, lugging a bucket in each hand, headed to the mob of calves in the farthest paddock. She tipped the milk into the feeding trough and manhandled the bossier young creatures to the outside teats, allowing the meeker ones to use the middle holder which flowed more quickly. The process was repeated with each pen of animals before the buckets were returned to the shed and flushed with boiling water, then she returned to each crib to scrub them clean.

In the late afternoon sun of early summer, it was a pleasant way to spend an hour or two each day. Thankfully, the greater portion of new calves occurred in the spring; Dawn knew her enjoyment would quite possibly fade if she had to do this job every day of the year. The discomfort of torrential downpours springing out of nowhere in autumn and winter, churning the ground to a quagmire, did nothing for her except to help her appreciate good weather when it came. A perfectly timed calving meant the regular stream of calves could fit in the long, narrow sheds at night and enjoy frolicking in fresh open pasture during the day.

"All done?" Charlie's weather-beaten face greeted

her at the vat as she dipped the billy into the frothy milk.

"Yep—another mob of happy customers." She grinned at him as he pushed his cloth hat back and scratched his balding scalp.

"See you tomorrow then," Charlie said.

Dawn unclipped Gyp and waved before trudging steadily up the slope and crossing the road to home. Her thoughts swept back to her mother as she walked, and Lillian's words repeated again and again in her head. She was struggling financially. Why hadn't she mentioned it before? Dawn had no idea what she spent her money on. Her understanding had always been that her mother made a good income as a dressmaker. In addition, her grandmother's inheritance, and her father's legacy in the form of a war widow's pension, should have been plenty to live on, shouldn't it? She shook her head. Her own earnings as a mobile hairdresser, plus the small income Charlie and Bev had provided since she'd been helping them, had filtered slowly into her account and the balance continued to grow. With the farm paying for almost everything else —the cars, fuel, food, and electricity—she had plenty to loan her mother or give her if she had needed it.

No. Perhaps this is the right thing for her to do. How old is she? Fifty? Sixty? Dawn was surprised to admit she had no idea—and would never dare ask.

———

F ITTING THE DESK INTO THE BOOT OF THE CAR HAD taken a good deal of care and organisation. That piece of furniture wasn't big, however, the cabinet that had once stored the 'unmentionable' bedtime chamber pot beside her grandmother's bed, and the box of her own toys, books, and remnants of her childhood filled a great deal more of the car than they had anticipated.

It was with an ache in her heart that they drove away from the sturdy, white-painted stucco home. Its lead-light windows and deep, shaded veranda seemed to close its eyes in sympathetic sorrow.

Dawn heaved a sigh and turned to her husband. "I hope Mum is happy. Not sure what else we can do?"

John squeezed her hand briefly, then released it as he negotiated the corner. "Nothing, love. It's hard to help someone who doesn't want help. Just be there for her when she calls."

Dawn shrugged and stared through the windscreen at the road ahead. Her mother had always been emotionally distant but knowing that didn't help. She had never understood why. The emptiness inside her grew.

<h1 style="text-align:center">CHAPTER 17</h1>

The dainty antique desk stood in the corner of the lounge for several days before Dawn decided to rearrange the furniture and position it under the side window near the fireplace. She paused to stare through the window, resting her elbows on the sill. The south side of the garden was filled with bulbs and brightly coloured lupins, which she had come to love so much. "You pretty little flowers are my talisman."

Beyond the house garden, the paddock sloped down to the road, and on the far side, a hill rose from the valley and overlooked the harbour. Remnants of terraces, once part of a fortified Maori settlement, were etched into its topmost rise, casting shadows against the green grass.

She returned her attention to the room and picked up the desk, tipping it toward her to settle it into a better position. As she lifted it, she heard something inside it slide, and she hastily set it down.

Bother. Don't tell me it's falling to pieces now.

She opened the drawers on either side and bent to inspect the contents. Nothing. Both were completely empty. *Mum definitely removed whatever she had stored inside them.* Dawn shrugged. *Probably just a loose screw.*

On the other side of the hearth, Dawn shuffled the small cabinet into position and placed the record player on top of it. The storage rack for her albums fitted neatly underneath where once a chamber pot would have rested. She stood back, hands on hips and gave a satisfied smile. *Perfect.*

She removed her writing pad, envelopes, and other office paraphernalia from the kitchen drawer, tidied them into an orderly pile, and carried them to the writing desk. Balancing the pile against her chest, she pulled the tiny knob on the drawer. It seemed reluctant to budge and she pulled again, her tug harder than she intended. The piece of furniture rocked on its thin, dainty legs.

Again, something moved inside, a soft sliding sound, and she frowned. Dropping to her knees, she placed her load on the floor and ran her hand underneath the desk. The surface was thicker than it looked and she explored further, astounded when her fingers touched on a tiny wooden clip under the desk's lid. She flicked it up and the lip of the desktop moved toward her. Sliding her index finger into the gap, she prised the opening wider—and a shallow drawer the width of the desk slid open.

Oh my goodness! A secret drawer?

A musty smell mixed with a hint of naphthalene rose to greet her, and she screwed up her nose. The drawer appeared empty but Dawn shoved her flattened hand inside it, groping along the edges to be sure. Her fingertips touched something soft and she squealed, withdrawing her hand, and catching it on the sharp edge as her imagination touched on possibilities. An old bag of herbs perhaps—or worse, a dead mouse? She pulled the drawer out as far as it would go and slid her hand in again. When she touched the object, she drew it toward her with one finger.

A tiny black velvet bag, no bigger than a coat button, greeted her, and she delicately pinched the drawstring and held it to the light. It weighed little more than a threepenny piece. She squeezed it between her fingers and was surprised to feel something round and hard inside. She prised the bag open and tipped the contents onto the green leather surface of the desk.

Her eyes widened as she stared at the beautiful gold ring with its single diamond and minute silver etching on either side of the stone. *An engagement ring.*

"Hello! I'm home." John's voice boomed down the hallway, and she abandoned the ring and rushed to greet him.

"Come and see what I've found." She grabbed him

by the hand, dragging him into the lounge and across to the desk. She pointed to her find and waited while he picked it up, fingering it gently before meeting her gaze.

"Whose is it?" he asked.

"I've no idea. I discovered it in a secret compartment in the desk that used to be my grandmother's. Mum has been using it for years, so maybe she knows something about it?"

"Hmm." John chuckled as he lay the ring back on the leather pad. "Good luck cross-examining her about that."

Dawn frowned. "You're right. What if it is Mum's? It can't be the ring Dad gave her because she never takes that off. And Gran always wore hers, too, before she died and bequeathed it to me. Anyway, we both know what it's like because I wear it whenever we go out."

"It probably belonged to some long-forgotten aunt or something. Whoever the owner was, or is, it's obviously yonks since it saw the light of day." John shrugged and placed it on the desk. "What's for lunch?"

She grimaced as she met his enquiring blue eyes. "Whoops. Nothing yet. I've been busy rearranging things here and lost track of time."

He laughed and lay his arm over her shoulders. "I'll make us a toasted sandwich while you find a safe spot for your precious treasure."

Poppy wound herself around Dawn's legs, and

Dawn picked her up and rubbed her face against the cat's soft fur. Poppy was now a feline matriarch as her first litter of three kittens had made themselves at home with John and Dawn. She tipped the cat onto her back and stroked her tummy, running her finger gently along the faded scar down her midline.

"Are you pleased you don't have to look after any more kittens, little one?" Dawn asked. The cat purred loudly and Dawn smiled. "Of course you do. Your operation may have been a bit tough, but there's a limit to how many feline friends we both need around here. Don't you agree?"

Carrying the cat, Dawn followed John to the kitchen and placed her on the squashy cushion at the end of the padded seat. Squeezing in beside her, Dawn watched John cut slices of cold mutton and prepare a pile of toasted cheese, meat, and tomato sandwiches.

The radio blared out "Hey Jude" and she smiled as John danced around the kitchen. Alice had been right when she had insisted her boys learn the roles usually performed by women, just as Alice had to do the jobs normally conducted by men on the farm. Dawn was proud of her own achievements and now considered herself capable of doing most things asked of her, indoors or out—in spite of the steep learning curve in the beginning and a few blazing rows.

John bent and kissed her on the cheek, and her heart swelled with love for her handsome husband. Life was pretty near perfect.

AFTER A TASTY LUNCH, DAWN ANNOUNCED HER SPUR-of-the-moment decision as she walked out to the gate with John. "I'm going to visit Ed and Hilde tomorrow."

"Nice. Give them my regards."

A horse was tethered under the pine tree near the garage, its head hanging low while it slept. As the gate clicked, it jumped to attention and nickered.

"I didn't realise you brought Honey home." Dawn reached up and stroked the chestnut mare's nose. "No wonder I didn't hear you arrive."

Fantail Ridge supported three horses although they were not ridden as frequently today as they had been the past. Harry preferred an aging brown gelding they called Rambler, while John loved the young mare he had purchased as a yearling, their bond growing as he educated her for use on the farm. The third was a geriatric Clydesdale called Major that had been a work horse following the war and throughout the decades. While the old gelding was stiff with arthritis and blind in one eye, even Dawn recognised the adoration he had for Alice. He lived in the house paddock with the cow and chooks, patiently waiting each morning for Alice's visit and carrot treats.

"Dad and I got the cattle shifted this morning, so I'm off to bring a mob of sheep into the yards now for drenching." John rubbed the mare's face before bending to tighten the girth. "Honey enjoys a day of action now and then, don't you, girl?"

He kissed Dawn then slid his foot into the stirrup and swung his leg over the saddle. "See you later."

She smiled as he turned and rode away at a brisk trot with Hoover, the young golden-coloured dog currently in training, loping along beside them.

For the rest of the day, Dawn's thoughts travelled regularly to the ring and her imagination explored all kinds of possibilities. Had her grandmother been engaged before she married her grandfather? Or had the ring belonged to someone a generation before her? Perhaps it was linked to a jilted bride—or worse, a dead one!

THE FOLLOWING MORNING, DAWN CLEARED THE breakfast dishes, hung a load of washing on the line, then picked up her bag of hairdressing equipment. She slid into the driver's seat and reversed the little Morris out of the garage. The day had dawned clear and bright, and in the early summer warmth, a wave of joy filled her heart. She burst into song, slapping her hands on the steering wheel and singing everything that came into her head as she drove north toward Ed's farm.

In recent weeks, she'd travelled around the district two or three mornings a week to cut the hair of her ever-growing clientele. After arriving home in time to have lunch with John and prepare the evening meal, she walked across the road to the dairy to feed the hoard of calves.

Her excitement increased as she neared the Hansen farm. It had been weeks since she'd last visited. Even four years on, Dawn limited her visits to once every month to ensure the family didn't feel too imposed upon.

For Dawn, befriending Hilde had been considerably easier than it had been for her to befriend Ed. It was as though once Hilde recovered from her journey and reacquainted herself with her long-lost brother, she realised how fortunate she had been when Dawn found her at the Helensville Railway Station. She confided in Dawn, admitting it hadn't occurred to her that New Zealand wouldn't have a boat or bus that would take her to the farm. In Norway, public transport was plentiful, especially ferries due to the hundreds of islands, fiords, and waterways.

Hilde was on her knees, weeding the flowerbed alongside the driveway as Dawn turned in the gate. She pushed herself to her feet and waved the small digging fork in greeting. Ahead, Ed's broad back was bent over a fallen branch, and his elbow swung rhythmically back and forth as he cut it into pieces with a handsaw.

Dawn parked on the lawn beside the drive and removed both her hairdressing bag and the jar of raspberry jam from the back seat. She held the jar out to

Hilde and dropped her bag on the ground as she was engulfed in a bear hug.

"It is very good to see you. A long time now," Hilde said.

"I know. I'm sorry I haven't been for a while. I've been helping Charlie and Bev with the spring calves, and you know what that's like." Dawn grinned as the older woman nodded fiercely. As if in response, the bellow of a young calf filled the air, and they both laughed.

"We have thirty babies now. Very busy," Hilde said.

Ed's beautiful jersey herd was less than half the size of Charlie's but, in Dawn's opinion, the smaller cream and gold cows with their huge brown eyes were much prettier. She couldn't imagine why they would need a bigger herd with just the two of them—especially as both Hilde and Ed must be in their late sixties or seventies by now.

"I'm looking forward to seeing them," she said.

Hilde nodded. "First we have tea, and then you cut our hair." She pulled off her hat and let the long, thin plait drop down her back.

Today, Dawn was filled with the mystery of the ring, and she shared it with the old couple as they sipped their tea.

"You must ask your mother." Hilde frowned, and Dawn's eyes widened in surprise. "Too many secrets are not good." She met her brother's gaze before diverting the conversation to the success of their most recent fishing expedition.

Their voices became a murmur in the background as Dawn dwelt on how on earth she could approach her mother. *I don't think this is a question for our Sunday phone call. There's nothing else for it—I will have to visit her.*

CHAPTER 18

"I suppose that will be alright. I don't have anything in my diary until Friday's bridge club."

Dawn released her breath silently and rolled her eyes. Switching the receiver to her other ear, she mustered a cheery reply. "Great. Don't worry about a thing, Mum. I'll bring my own linen and enough food for both of us. Is there anything else you need?"

A five-second silence met Dawn's question before Lillian sighed heavily. "No, I don't think so. I'll see you tomorrow morning then—unless you change your mind."

"I won't—and I'll stay just the one night," Dawn finished firmly.

"Goodbye then. See you tomorrow," Lillian replied and hung up.

"Hmm. Okay, bye to you too." Dawn looked at the receiver and placed it back into the cradle.

Reaching into the corner, she switched the record player on and pulled the Bee Gees record from its sleeve. Then, with the volume turned up, and singing along with the music, Dawn busied herself in the kitchen, baking shortbread, fruit cake, a meat loaf, and two shepherd's pies. She glanced at Poppy curled in a ball on the bench seat.

"That should keep John happy while I'm away—and be enough for Mum and me. We'll see if she appreciates it."

The cat opened one eye as if to say *doubtful*, and Dawn laughed.

———

JOHN LEANED THROUGH THE WINDOW AND KISSED HER again. "Now, don't get too upset with her. No point in burning bridges. Drive carefully and look out for idiots on those city roads."

She smiled at him and gave a slight shake of her head. "Of course, sweetheart. I'll be fine. I'll ring you if there's any change but I should be back before dark tomorrow."

He stood back as she changed into first gear and moved away, a smile firmly plastered on her face. With the exception of those who lived on the farm and those who drove locally, John's opinion of all other drivers seemed to be that they were incompetent fools who couldn't follow rules and shouldn't be behind the wheel. She half expected him to find fault with her driving. Luckily for him, he hadn't.

Waving out the window, she glanced in the rear-vision mirror and her heart gave a lurch. John remained by the gate with Gyp at his side as the two of them watched her drive away. In more than five years of marriage, this would be the first night she had been without him, and shock reverberated through her body. She felt as though a piece of her was being left behind.

Concentrating on the road, Dawn pushed all thoughts of home aside and ran through the myriad ways she could broach the subject of the ring with her mother.

Arriving outside the row of brick flats, her stomach did a somersault, and she drew a deep breath. It felt strange knowing it was her mother's home … and yet it was bore no resemblance to the home she'd known.

"Right, let's do this." She reached into the back seat and hauled out her suitcase, slung her bag over her shoulder, and locked the car.

———

THE NEAT AND COMPACT UNIT WAS UNFAMILIAR, THE only hints of home being the clock on the kitchen wall and the Constable print in its wooden frame in the lounge. Dawn kissed her mother's cool cheek and hovered awkwardly. Lillian appeared not to notice, ushering her daughter down the tiny hallway and into the spare bedroom. At the sight of her old bookend bedhead, relief flooded Dawn, even if the new quilt in her mother's favourite shade of lilac brought a smirk to her face. Dutifully following her mother back to the lounge, she issued positive comments she knew would appease Lillian. While Dawn unpacked the food, Lillian launched into a detailed monologue about the neighbours, her prowess at the bridge club, and finally, Dawn's friend Ann, who Lillian had apparently bumped into the day before at the new supermarket down the road.

"She's dying to see you. Did you know her husband is doing well and now has quite a large business? I see his signs all over the suburb, outside construction sites. Oh, and she's given birth to her fourth child? Imagine that. I told her you'd pop down to visit in the morning before you go home."

Dawn nodded, manufacturing a smile. She, too, wanted to catch up with her old friend. However, she doubted her mother would understand her fear of a busy household with four young children—like a slap in the face, exaggerating Dawn's own barrenness. Dawn would go, but this was different to visiting Jill and Tom. They were family—when once, Ann and Dawn had trod a similar path. She'd thought they'd do everything together.

Struggling to eat lunch as the butterflies completed their somersaults in her stomach, Dawn let her eyes wander subtlety toward the woman opposite her. A little taller than Alice, Lillian only reached the top of Dawn's ears. Dawn had assumed her height came from her father's side of the family. Lillian's grey-blue eyes and mousey brown hair contrasted with Dawn's hazel eyes and her blonde locks. Broaching any subject about her family history had always been difficult— as though there was something to hide, something that couldn't or wouldn't be spoken about. *Perhaps I was adopted? No siblings and a big difference between Mum's and my features?*

It was almost mid-afternoon before she summoned the courage to place a cup of tea on the table in front of her mother and draw the tiny velvet bag from her pocket. She shook the ring onto the cloth and pulled out the opposite chair.

Lillian reached out before snatching her hand away again, as though the ring was on fire.

"Where did you get this?" Her voice was low, and Dawn had to lean forward to hear her properly.

"I found it in Gran's desk. It was hidden in a secret drawer that I found by chance."

Her mother raised her head and stared at her, her face drained of colour and her eyes wide. She opened her mouth as though to speak, and then closed it again while she stared at the table.

"Did you put it there?" Dawn sat up straighter, concern flooding her as Lillian shrank in her chair and her face crumpled. She reached out and touched her mother's arm. "Are you alright? Have I upset you?"

Lillian straightened and met Dawn's gaze, her own eyes pools of sadness. "I should have known this would surface one day."

"Is this yours or Gran's?"

"It was mine. I gave it to your gran to put somewhere safe because I couldn't bear the pain of seeing it." She sat back in her chair and dropped her head forward, whispering, "The love of my life gave it to me before he left for war. We were to wed when he returned."

Dawn sat in stunned silence while she digested her mother's revelation. Something in her tone suggested her mother was not talking about her deceased husband, but Dawn had to be sure. "D-do you mean my father?"

Lillian shook her head and placed the ring in the palm of her hand, stroking it gently before attempting to slide it onto her left ring finger. When it reached the second knuckle, the ring could go no farther, and Lillian appeared to study her two engagement rings, her chin quivering a little before she spoke. "No. He was your father's best friend."

Dawn narrowed her eyes in confusion, waiting for an explanation. When it didn't come, she prompted her mother. "And?"

"His name was Peter. He was in the same regiment as your father, and they fought side by side in Asia.

Peter was killed when they were captured by the Japanese and your father imprisoned in Changi."

Dawn sucked in a breath. The mention of Changi prison brought horror to most New Zealanders, and although it had only been touched on briefly in school history lessons, it had been enough to bring silent respect to all students. Dawn had no idea her own father had been captured. "How on earth did he survive that?"

Lillian shook her head slowly. "I don't know. We didn't know Peter had died for months, and by the time the news came through, the war was over. I was heartbroken and have few memories of those days. When your father got home, he came to see me. He was kind and understanding and after several visits, he told me that Peter had asked him to take care of me. We became good friends, and although our love was different, he was kind and caring. That was when I knew it was time to take the ring off, and your grandmother said she would take care of it."

Dawn rose and made a fresh cup of tea for them both. The skinny black hands of the kitchen clock pointed to twenty past four. She glanced back at her mother, and her head swirled with emotion.

Placing the fresh pot of tea on the table, she laid her hand gently on her mother's shoulder. Lillian reached up and clasped it, and Dawn stood motionless for several minutes.

"Come on, Mum. The tea will be getting cold."

Oblivious to the hot drink, Lillian continued softly, gaining purpose as she poured out the history that Dawn had longed to hear all her life. "Your father never really recovered from Changi though. The starvation and torture he'd lived through had caused so much damage. Neither his heart nor mind could cope."

While her mother drew a deep breath and stared into space, Dawn searched the recesses of her memory unsuccessfully as she tried to remember her father. Lillian continued, jolting her back to the present and Dawn abandoned her thoughts, desperate to hear more.

"You were such a tiny scrap of a baby. Much too early, and I was too sick to care for you. Your gran looked after us all. Lord knows how. My own father had died only weeks before and she had enough to worry about." Her face slackened and Dawn was consumed with sadness. In ten short minutes, her mother seemed to have aged ten years. "I haven't been a very good mother."

It may have been true, but a sudden awareness of the shift in their relationship strengthened Dawn, and she replied firmly, "You mustn't think like that."

The two of them were all that was left of an already small and fractured family, and Dawn wasn't about to allow that to disintegrate completely.

"I think we need a walk in the fresh air. It's cooling off now and will be a lovely evening." Dawn reached for her mother's hand, surprised when Lillian took it and rose to her feet. Dawn placed a light cardigan around her mother's shoulders and picked up the house keys, and together, they walked down the road.

Silence enveloped them both until they reached the park. Children threw bread to the ducks as they quacked and bickered around the pond, and Dawn smiled.

"I remember when I was little, Gran used to bring me here sometimes. I always wanted you to come, but you were too busy." Dawn kept her voice light, worried that this newfound comradeship was fleeting and could be easily shattered.

"I know. I am sorry now I didn't make more effort. I never seemed to have the energy, and as long as your grandmother was alive, I didn't have to worry. I knew she would love you and care for you more than I could." Lillian's pale face met her daughter's and again, shock stabbed at Dawn as a tear slid down her mother's cheek.

Tucking Lillian's hand more firmly into her elbow, Dawn guided her around the pathway edging the park. Taking care to steer her away from the dog walkers and young couples marching jovially along with children in tow, she quietly asked her mother about her own childhood, her happiness—and finally, what had been the reason for her lack of siblings.

"After you, the doctor said I mustn't have any more children." Lillian shrugged. "Anyway, your father got sick when you were only a toddler, so there was no chance of considering increasing the family, even if I had been able to."

Dawn was sure her heart would crack as compassion and understanding seeped through her body. "I've never had the chance to tell you, but I, too, have lost two babies now. One was when I went to hospital in that first year after we were married. The other was a couple of years ago, and if I have conceived again since then, it hasn't been obvious and I must have miscarried very early."

This time, it was Lillian who clutched Dawn's hand tightly, and a quiet sympathy transferred to her daughter. "You're young. There is still time. You also have a kind and healthy husband, so you must not give up hope."

Dawn nearly fell over backwards. It was the first time ever that Lillian had touched on such a personal topic with her daughter, and for a moment, words stuck in Dawn's throat.

"Will you come and join us for Christmas this year, Mum?" Dawn asked.

Lillian paused for a moment before speaking. "Do you know, I think that would be very nice."

She squeezed her mother's hand and grinned. "I'll take you to see the lupin fields while they're still flowering. It's the most beautiful sight you can imagine."

The sun dipped in the sky as they reached the park gate and turned for home, its mellow warmth soaking into Dawn's shoulders easing the shock of the afternoon's revelations.

———

THE FOLLOWING MORNING, FOR THE FIRST TIME IN HER life, it was Lillian who brought Dawn her early cup of tea in bed.

"Thanks, Mum." Dawn smiled, relieved to see colour back in her mother's face, the previously deep lines that made her appear so stern now softer and less noticeable.

It seems unloading long-held secrets can be good for your health.

"As soon as we've eaten breakfast, why don't you pop up to Ann's place, and I'll wash up and read the paper? Then, when you get back, we'll have early lunch and you can get home before John starts to worry."

Dawn gave her mother a tiny nod, wary of this new, gentler Lillian. *Will it last?*

Standing on the porch of the half-painted house, Dawn hesitated. She had pushed the doorbell to no avail, waited a minute, and then knocked briskly on the glass panel beside the heavy wooden door. Raised voices echoed inside, a young child's cries and the gentle soothing voice of a woman. Ann? She lifted her hand to knock again as the door opened, and time stood still.

"Dawn! Lovely to see you." Ann stepped forward,

attempting to hug her friend with one arm while the other hitched a toddler higher on her hip. "Come in."

Her friend oozed the same warmth that had drawn Dawn to her in primary school, and Dawn was pleased she had come. Stepping around scattered toys and a bulky metal toolbox, she navigated her way behind Ann along the hall and into a large and open kitchen and living area.

"Sorry about the mess. Graham's been working on our house ever since we moved in. You know what it's like. If you're married to an electrician, your own place is always blowing fuses or needing bulbs replaced. And as you can see, when you're married to a builder, your home comes last in the order of priorities." She laughed and swept the clutter, dirty dishes and half-eaten food on the bench into the sink with her free arm before switching the tap on and filling the kettle.

"Would you like me to do something to help?" Dawn cast a helpless glance around, glimpsing two small children playing with a dog in the back garden, their shrieks drifting through the open window.

"Here, you take her, and I'll make us a cuppa while the baby is asleep and life is relatively quiet." Ann handed the little girl to her and Dawn tucked her awkwardly on her hip. *What is it like when not quiet?*

"What's her name?" Dawn asked, cuddling the toddler closer.

"That's Amy. The baby's called Oliver, and those two ratbags outside are Brian and Mary. They're all named after grandparents, so everyone's happy." Ann laughed again and Dawn grinned.

"Do you get much help from any of them? The grandparents, I mean." She cast her eyes around the room, staring with envy at the mountain of what looked like clean laundry overflowing from a huge wicker basket. *I wouldn't mind having to deal with that if I had these beautiful children.*

"A little. Mum comes over once a week and gets to the bottom of the ironing pile, and Graham's mum likes us to go there every Sunday for the family dinner so it saves me having to cook at least once a week." She heaved a sigh, attempting an apologetic smile. "I promise it's not usually this bad. It's just that the baby has had a cold, so I've been struggling to keep up to date—and I'm always so tired."

"Aww. You poor thing." Dawn studied the dark circles under her friend's eyes, and the long, lank hair that hung over her shoulders, crying out for a wash and a trim.

"Look at me. I'm still in my old duds because I haven't had time for a shower yet." Ann gave a brief, self-conscious giggle, and Dawn's chest squeezed with sympathy.

"Would you like to shower now? I can watch the children for you." Familiarity and care for her old friend swept away the last of her reservations. *After all, children can't be too different from animals, can they?.*

"Really? That would be fabulous."

The cup of tea forgotten, Ann dashed down the hall, and Dawn's attention reverted to the little girl clinging to her with one hand while she sucked the thumb of the other.

Two hours later, Dawn parked outside her mother's unit again and breathed out slowly. Perhaps things were the way they were meant to be. Her desire for a big family had been crushed by Mother Nature. Now, she'd become accustomed to her quiet, orderly home with her beloved husband. The short, exhausting bursts of family life with her friend's children and John's nephews and niece filled any void quite satisfactorily.

With surprise, she realised divulging the news of the ring and her own mother's revelations, so important to Dawn, had been forgotten. She couldn't be certain that Ann had even registered the change in relationship between her mother and Dawn or how much that meant to Dawn. The sharing of secrets between friends had shifted, and Ann's own family came first for her—as it should.

And Dawn couldn't wait to go home to John.

CHAPTER 19

Christmas, 1971, was like no other for Dawn. A bright summer day with only the hint of a breeze promised to be the perfect condition for an outdoor celebration, and excitement spread through her veins. While at times it was difficult to comprehend that her mother was the same woman who had visited Fantail Ridge years before, Lillian occasionally reverted to the cold, stern woman Dawn remembered, forcing Dawn to creep around the house as though on eggshells. She hoped that today would not be one of those.

She need not have worried. Today, she appeared to be the 'new' Lillian, and with purpose in her stride, she donned her walking shoes and accompanied Dawn to the dairy farm as the summer sun peeped over the horizon, spreading its pink and apricot rays across the sky. Although wary of the animals, Lillian's attempts to hide her fear were obvious and Dawn sympathised with her, taking every opportunity to protect her and ensure she enjoyed her stay. While adjusting to the subtle changes in Lillian, Dawn nevertheless allowed her expectations to remain in neutral in case the bubble burst and their relationship returned to the way it had always been. *Lunch with the tribe will be the real test.*

With an ancient tent pitched on the lawn and a stack of chairs spread in a horseshoe shape around the trestle tables, there was ample seating for the extended family and friends expected for the day. Alice bustled back and forth from the kitchen, throwing instructions at anyone who caught her eye and wiping perspiration from her brow with her apron. Accepting Lillian's offer of help, Alice subtly suggested setting the tables would be great, and Dawn met their host's gaze as they returned to the house.

"Thanks for making her feel included." She gave Alice an appreciative smile.

Alice silently reached out and squeezed Dawn's arm.

By mid-morning, jugs of lemonade and rhubarb cordial, clinking with ice, were placed out of the sun's increasingly hot rays in the shade of the tent. Dawn placed glasses on the white tablecloth as the last of the family arrived at the farm, leaping joyfully from their vehicles in a noisy rabble.

In the years since Dawn's move to South Head, John's niece and nephews seemed to have doubled in height, and their individual personalities both intrigued and delighted their aunty. Paul, a lanky, spotty, younger version of George, gave her a shy hug before revealing the telescope in the box he carried and launching into a description of its amazing abilities. Her heart reached out to him as his voice croaked and squeaked between that of a man's and a boy's, and his face reddened. Cara had blossomed into a pretty, confident teenager, twirling her ponytail with one hand while she took command of the youngest in the crew, Richard, who appeared desperate to climb the trees with his older brothers. In turn, Tim and Jill's children had greeted each adult politely for two seconds, throwing their arms around their grandparents briefly before acknowledging the nod from their father and taking off across the lawn.

"They don't change, do they." Jill laughed and handed the bowl of fruit salad to Alice. "I'll get the pavlova out of the car."

"Let me help." Dawn strode to the vehicle with her sister-in-law and reached into the boot to retrieve the delicately wrapped dessert. Jill's head dived under the raised boot door and she whispered furtively, "How's your mother? Is she still a changed woman?"

Dawn chuckled and raised her eyebrows. "Mostly. I can't believe it, actually. Something has transformed between us since I found that ring, and she's finally begun to treat me more as a friend and less like a nuisance. It's good and I still can't believe it, but I'm making the most of our time together to strengthen what we now have—and I hope we never return to the way we were."

"Well, you've got a lot of catching up to do and I'm happy for you." Jill closed the door and picked up the bag of swimming gear from the ground. "We brought these with us in the hope we can go for a swim before we head home tonight. Tim said the tide will be perfect."

Dawn smiled widely. "Great idea."

———

AS THE CLOCK TICKED TOWARD MIDDAY, THE conversations grew louder and more jovial, halting only when the growl of an engine signalled another visitor. Car doors slammed, and the younger boys raced to the gate to greet Ed and Hilde as they entered the yard, closely followed by a middle-aged couple.

"Clive! Jean! Lovely to see you both again." Alice hugged each of the adults in turn before leading them across the lawn. The rest of the family jostled and reached out to shake hands and bestow hugs and kisses on their long-term friends while Susan glided toward them carrying a tray of cold drinks.

Dawn handed a glass to each person as the air swelled with laughter, sprinkled with the excitement of those whose social life was constrained by the long hours required in farming. Although she didn't know the older couple very well, Clive and Jean were valued friends and not a single Christmas had passed on Fantail Ridge without them popping in for a quick drink and a "hello" with Harry and Alice.

"We can't stay long," Clive said.

"Our daughter told us we were to be at her place no later than half past twelve." Jean giggled, and Alice pressed her hand against her mouth. Dawn remembered hearing that Clive and Jean were not the best time-keepers, and those who knew them well had developed the habit of giving them a start time at least an hour before everyone else.

True to their word, Clive and Jean swallowed their drinks and waved goodbye with almost enough time to get to Helensville for lunch with their family— if they drove at breakneck speed. Following their departure, the women gathered in the kitchen, slicing ham and roast turkey, dishing up trays of vegetables and stirring gravy while outside, the children kicked the football around the garden, and Harry's raised voice carried across the lawn.

"If your gran catches you kicking that ball anywhere near the delphiniums, there'll be trouble."

He needn't have wasted his breath as the threat received a brief shrug and was otherwise ignored.

Consuming the huge, delicious meal was almost as

exhausting as cleaning up afterwards, and by mid-afternoon, even the children seemed content to lie on the rug under the tree, reading books and playing cards with barely a bicker. Richard rested his head against Gyp's outstretched belly while Cara read aloud to him, and Dawn cast a glance toward her mother, smiling at her bowed head in the comfy garden seat. Her hat had slipped over her eyes and her arm hung by her side, her small, dainty hand almost touching the freshly cut grass. Alice's feet were raised on the stool opposite her as she lay against the sloping back of a chair that matched Lillian's, her eyes closed and her mouth slack.

Dawn nudged Susan with her foot as she lay on the rug next to her. "Do you reckon that'll be us in a few more years?"

Susan smiled and Jill grimaced, leaning toward her, and whispering. "Probably—and I don't think it's too far away." She yawned and closed her eyes.

As the afternoon stretched out, the sun moved toward the west and a breeze blew off the harbour, stirring the dozing adults and invigorating the children.

"Can we go swimming now?" Mark's voice pierced the air, and within a few minutes, everyone was alert and struggling to their feet.

"We need to go home to milk the cows," Ed's deep voice rumbled as he reached out to help Hilde to her feet.

"I'll drive you," John offered while Dawn and Susan

moved to the table and began collecting the empty glasses.

Alice followed them into the kitchen, hastily opening the fridge and extracting the remnants of Christmas pudding. "Ed and Hilde are not going home without taking some of these leftovers. Wasn't the home-cured ham they brought us delicious?"

Dawn nodded. She was the one who had struggled to rearrange the food that was weighing down the shelves. How on earth would they get through it?

"Right. Well, I suggest that as soon as we've said goodbye to Ed and Hilde, Jill, you, and Susan worry about organising the children for the beach. Dawn and Lillian can help me put a picnic together to take with us." Alice looked up at the women milling around the kitchen and smiled.

"I would love to help," Lillian said. Behind her back, Jill's eyes widened and she shot Dawn a small grin before grabbing Susan's arm and heading outside.

———

GENTLE WAVES LAPPED THE SAND IN THE TINY BAY, AND the children shrieked and leapt as they ran into the sparkling water while their mothers hitched their skirts up and stood in the shallows.

"I'm in if you are." Jill turned her smiling face to Dawn, standing still at the water's edge.

In a daydream, remembering the first time she had

stood here during summer on Fantail Ridge, Dawn started and smiled back.

"Sure. Race you both in." She peeled her dress over her head, revealing a plain black one-piece swimsuit, then ran past the young women, throwing herself under the water in a neat, long dive. She swam several strokes farther out and rolled onto her back.

The water caressed her hot skin and she revelled in its fresh, salty smoothness, silently sending thanks to her grandmother who had insisted she learn to swim from a young age. The moods of the harbour could be fierce and unpredictable but on rare days like this, Dawn allowed the sea's gentleness to seep into her bones and she relaxed.

Her peace lasted less than a minute before the children drew near, splashing and laughing as they took turns to climb onto Paul's shoulders and leap into the sea. She glanced toward the sand, surprised to see Alice and Lillian paddling at the water's edge, their heads bowed as though in deep conversation. Farther along the beach, George and John had begun to build a bonfire and in the distance, Dawn caught a glance of Harry's back as he dragged an old fencepost out of the long grass. Jill's dip appeared to be over and she now lay sprawled on a towel while Susan stood knee deep in the water, clutching her wide brimmed hat with the tips of long fingers as she focused on the children.

Dawn swam toward her and hauled herself out of

the water. "Looks as though it'll be sausages and marshmallows for tea tonight."

Susan groaned. "Great. I don't think I could fit anything more in—but I can always try."

Pink stretches of thin cloud glowed and faded to purple as the sun set and the extended Simpson family gathered around the bonfire. Huddled together with towels draped around their shoulders, the children each held a long piece of wire with a marshmallow threaded onto the end of it. Dawn leaned against her husband as he placed his arm tightly around her.

"Hasn't it been a wonderful day?" he whispered. "Not a single argument."

Dawn glanced at her mother, sitting on a small folding stool next to Alice. As though she could feel her daughter's gaze, Lillian turned her head toward her, a wide smile transforming her face, and Dawn thought her heart would melt with happiness.

"The best ever," she whispered in return and crossed her fingers behind her back.

CHAPTER 20

Dawn pushed her dresses aside in the wardrobe, studying them one by one. "Which of you should I wear to the dance tonight?"

The sultry days of the Christmas week had disintegrated into a cold front bringing winds and blustery showers over the peninsula. Although it would be warm inside the hall, Dawn knew the soft blue sleeveless dress she had worn to the previous New Year's Eve dance wouldn't cut it in this weather.

"I guess it'll have to be you." She pulled a multi-coloured cotton frock from the cupboard and laid it on the bed. The shirred waistline and elbow-length sleeves would offer just enough warmth without being too hot —that was if John had enough energy left to dance.

She sighed and wandered to the window. Leaning her elbows on the sill, she stared across the land, squinting through the sheet of rain in the hope that the truck carrying her husband would magically materialise. John and Harry were top-dressing the paddocks nearest the woolshed, once again hoping that another coat of fertiliser would boost the feed and encourage a good price for this season's lambs. With wool prices falling steadily, farmers around the country were clutching at anything to help maintain financial balance, even if it took every daylight hour.

Within minutes, the rain stopped and Dawn grinned as the clouds cleared and sunshine glistened on the puddles. She snatched up a coat and slipped her gumboots on while leaning against the porch rail. She nudged the old dog with her toe. "Come on, girl. We're going for a walk to see how the men are getting on."

Gyp stretched and wagged her tail before mooching after her mistress while Sandy bounded around the pair of them. As she passed the kennels, Dawn unclipped Hoover before she and the dogs followed the shortcut across the grass. She paused at the bush track leading to the bottom of the hill and focused on the distant tractor circumnavigating the hay shed in the paddock beyond the woolshed. Closer to her, the fertiliser pit, with its concrete walls and corrugated iron roof neatly tucked into the hillside, had its doors wide open while a blue front-end loader wove back and forth into its depths. She strode down the hill, emerging onto the lush pastures of the flat before climbing the slope toward the workers. Stopping to catch her breath, she squinted at the red tractor, now turning tight, continuous circles two paddocks away while grey clouds formed a bank along the horizon.

"That's weird. If he's empty, wouldn't he be driving back to get another load?" Dawn asked.

The dogs stopped and glanced at her, Gyp's head tilted to one side as if trying to understand the question.

Dawn increased her pace. Something deep in her gut stirred and her pulse quickened. "John! John!"

She ran around the side of the fertiliser bin, waving her arms to attract her husband's attention. His mouth opened in surprise as he switched off the engine and raised his hand.

"Hello. I didn't expect a visit today." He narrowed his eyes as she shook her head.

"What's Harry doing on the tractor?"

"What do you mean? He's got the spreader going, and I'm about to load it for the last time—I hope."

"The tractor's going 'round in little circles."

John swung his legs around and leapt off the seat in one swift movement, rushing behind the vehicle for a better look.

"Something's wrong!" John rarely raised his voice, and at his yell, Dawn's heart raced.

He took off, his long legs covering the ground at speed, his heavy boots hammering into the mud while the two younger dogs galloped beside him. Dawn sprinted behind, memories of her school athletic days at the forefront of her mind, and she leaned forward and pushed harder while Gyp remained flopped on the grass next to the pit.

"Don't worry about the gates." John flung the first one open as Dawn caught up with him, pausing momentarily before they increased the pace again. The distance between them closed quickly until John stopped and put his arm out to Dawn, preventing her from getting too close to the tractor. Harry appeared to be concentrating, his hands clutching the steering wheel, oblivious to their presence—or the fact that he was driving in continuous and pointless circles.

"Dad!"

Harry turned his head toward them slowly, recognition and surprise registering on his face.

"I'll jump on. Stay there." John ran beside the vehicle and swung himself onto the steel step. Reaching across the steering wheel, he thumped the kill switch and the tractor ground to a halt.

With her heart pounding, Dawn took some deep breaths, watching in horror as Harry's lips opened and shut in an attempt to speak. As the roar of the engine died completely, a jumble of muddled sounds dribbled from the man's mouth.

"Dad! What's wrong?" John pushed Harry back into the seat while Dawn clambered up the opposite side of the tractor. "Talk to me."

Harry stared into John's face and once again, attempted a conversation, his words sliding out, slurred and senseless. Dawn released Harry's hand from the steering wheel. It fell limply to his side and she gasped. She picked it up and rubbed his rough, cold fingers between hers.

"Let's get you home, Dad." John leaned against his father and started the engine again. "Dawn, make sure he doesn't topple. I'll do my best to drive."

With the three of them squeezed into the space designed for one, they lurched across the paddock toward the house, halting at the road gate.

"Help me get him out of the tractor and then you run ahead and get Mum," John said.

Dawn didn't look back, instead flying down the gravel to the homestead as fast as her gumboots would carry her. Panting hard, she leaned against the door of the back room and called out, "Alice. We need you. Harry's not good."

The kitchen door flew open and Alice gaped at Dawn while she dried her hands on her apron. "What's happened?"

"We don't know. He was driving in circles, and he can't speak properly or lift one arm."

"Oh Lord. It could be a stroke." Alice kicked off her slippers and shoved her feet into her boots. By the time they reached the front gate, John and Harry were only a few metres away, and both women rushed to assist them. Harry's left leg trailed along the ground while John half carried, half dragged his father to the garden seat outside the house. Alice held her husband's face between her hands.

"What have you done this time, you old turkey?" Her voice shook in spite of her playful words, and Dawn was sure her heart would crack.

"What shall I do?" Dawn shot John an anxious look.

"I think we'd better get him in to the hospital. Can you get the keys from the office and reverse Mum and Dad's car out of the shed? We'll put him in the back seat and make him comfortable. I'll stay with him. Mum, you grab a bag with a few essentials in it for both of you. I suspect he'll have to stay in for a bit—at least until we know what's going on."

Dawn nodded and hurried inside again, her hand on Alice's arm. Alice disappeared into the hallway while Dawn grabbed the keys from the hook and sped back to the row of vehicle sheds in the yard. Sliding behind the wheel of the big car, she straightened her shoulders and pushed the clutch to the floor. The only vehicle she was accustomed to driving was her little Morris—and as this monster leapt into life, she swallowed her fear and reversed slowly onto the driveway.

Dawn left the engine running while she jumped out, picked up the bag and stowed it in the boot. Alice and John installed Harry in the back seat before Alice slid in beside him, tucking a blanket around his shoulders.

"You'll be fine love. I'm here with you." Alice's voice quavered.

While John hurried to the driver's seat, Dawn

leaned into the back and kissed Alice's cheek, alarmed at her pallor. Harry's eyes were shut and Dawn closed the car door carefully, her heart beating like a drum.

"Are you both alright there?" John turned his head as he spoke to his parents.

"We'll be fine. Please get us to the hospital as soon as you can." Alice's voice was barely a whisper and Dawn stepped back, urging John on with a wave.

"Don't worry about me. I'll ring the hospital and let them know you're coming then wait for your phone call, hopefully with good news." Dawn spoke with more confidence than she felt.

As the vehicle pulled away, John yelled out the window. "Mum's left a casserole in the oven!"

Dawn waved in acknowledgement. "I'll sort it!"

She remained stationary until the car disappeared around the bend and headed down the hill. She slumped against the shed wall. Her legs shook, and she waited a few moments, sucking in long, slow breaths. Then, straightening her shoulders, she pushed herself forward and stumbled into the house.

The tantalising smell of lamb casserole greeted Dawn as she slid open the kitchen door and her mouth watered. As if on cue, a sudden shower lashed the roof and rain trickled down the kitchen windowpane.

Snatching the receiver from its hook, she wound the handle rapidly and waited while the exchange plugged her through to the hospital. Reassured that her message had been understood by the matron, she drank a glass of cold tap water and headed through the boot room to the outside door.

"Well, dogs. It's just you and me now, so we'd better get on with it."

Having finally reached the homestead at her own pace, Gyp thumped her tail and shook herself, sprinkling Dawn with a shower of hairy drops while ignoring Hoover's enthusiasm as he bounced around her, urging her to play.

Dawn hovered in the doorway as the rain continued to fall. "It looks like I'd better see what needs doing inside before we tackle the outdoor chores."

As though understanding every word, Gyp yawned and slapped her tail once more before resuming her position on the doormat.

Dawn cleaned the kitchen, washed the baking utensils and opened the fridge to put the milk jug away. One shelf was filled with plates of delicate club sandwiches and pink jelly-coated lamingtons. *Of course. Alice has been cooking for tonight's dance, and now it will be the last thing on her mind.*

While she waited for the shower to clear, Dawn checked the casserole was cooked through and removed it from the oven to cool while she folded the basket of washing sitting on the couch. Anxious to get back to her little house before John rang, she glanced through the window again and twisted her lips.

"Come on, dogs. We're going to have to do the chores in the rain." Shrugging herself into her oilskin, she slipped her feet back into her gumboots and smiled at Gyp. "Thank goodness the cow is close to calving so we don't have to worry about milking her."

Grabbing the bucket of scraps from the bench, she closed the door behind her and wove her way through the gate behind the machinery shed. The neat little paddock housed the fowl run, cow bail, and the row of well-used dog kennels, and as she fed the chooks and collected the eggs, her mind flashed back to the paddock and the open fertiliser bin. *Should I close the doors in case the rain blows in?* Deciding it would be better to be safe than sorry, she secured the pen behind her and hurried back to the house, depositing the empty bucket in the boot room tub.

"Come on. We're not finished yet." The dogs followed her out into the rain again and Dawn sighed. Weariness and perhaps a tiny bit of shock, was setting in, slowing her pace.

After crossing the road, she made her way to the concrete store that held the year's supply of superphosphate and lime. Relieved to find the front-end loader tucked inside and clear of the entrance, she moved to the far end of the sliding door and leaned her full weight on it. It refused to budge. She pushed harder, grunting with exertion until the heavy timber gave way with a jerk. Stumbling after it, Dawn eased the pressure until it slid along the overhead track and nudged the framework on the opposite end of the doorway.

She rubbed the muscles at the base of her neck,

staring at Harry's tractor, now washed clean by the rain. Uncertainty hitched her breath. Having never driven the vehicle, Dawn contemplated whether or not this was a good time to learn. *No, the last thing John needs is to come home and find I've crashed the tractor.*

"Come on, dogs. I think we're done."

The rain stopped, and a glimmer of sunshine filtered through the clouds. Dawn frowned at the horizon. Daylight was fading fast, and her car was safely parked in the garage at home—more than a mile away as the crow flew. Walking home held no appeal after the events of the afternoon, and Alice wouldn't mind if she borrowed her car. At the thought of three muddy dogs in the back of the neat little vehicle, Dawn rummaged in the freezer, locating a bag of juicy bones, and added a cup full of dog biscuits to the enamel bowls she found under the sink. With her four-legged friends following her enthusiastically, she tied them to the extended chains attached to each of the kennels and placed the food in front of them. The rain had topped up the water containers and she gave them all a rub behind the ears.

"Good dogs. You're in charge here now. I'll be back in the morning to get you."

Returning inside, she stared at the casserole hungrily. Anticipating Alice's approval, she spooned half the contents into a container to take home and put the remainder in the fridge, then closed the back door firmly behind her. Minutes later, she halted the car outside her home, remaining in the vehicle as a wave of trepidation crept over her.

She stared at the darkened sky and slumped against the back of the seat. Tomorrow was the beginning of a new year. *What will 1972 bring? Is this a sign of what lies ahead?*

CHAPTER 21

The air was still and silent as she collected the container of food and walked up the path. As she opened the door, the phone began to ring. Her heart leapt. She paused to listen to the code, *long, short, long, short*, then hastily kicked off her boots, raced into the kitchen, and grabbed the receiver. "Hello?"

"It's me. Are you alright?"

At the sound of John's voice, Dawn collapsed onto the kitchen stool, weak with relief. "Yes, I'm fine. What's happening with Harry?" Her voice wavered with apprehension.

"They said Dad's had a stroke, but luckily, we acted quickly. His speech is clearer now and they've taken him in the ambulance to Auckland Hospital for tests."

"How's your mum?"

"Not too bad. She's gone with Dad, and I've rung George so he and Susan can meet them at the hospital."

Blood pounded in Dawn's chest. Was Harry's life in danger? "W-will he die?"

"I hope not. I suppose we'll know more once he's been examined by the experts. In the meantime, I'll be on my way home in a few minutes."

"Good. I've fed the chooks and tied the dogs up at the kennels so you don't need to stop—oh, and I borrowed your Mum's car to come home. I didn't think she'd mind."

"Thanks, sweetheart. No, of course she wouldn't. I'll swing in and swap the car for the truck and see you in an hour or so."

Words caught in her throat, and she barely managed to say goodbye. So many questions, so many possibilities. As she placed the receiver back in its cradle, a wave of nausea washed over her as disinfectant and bright lights flashed through her mind. She shuddered at her own hospital memories. Poor Harry. Hesitantly, she rose to her feet.

After a bowl of Alice's tasty stew and a full mug of tea, Dawn put the dirty dishes in the sink feeling infinitely better. She meandered into the lounge and glanced into their bedroom. Her brightly coloured dress seemed to taunt her as it lay on the bed. Picking it up, she held it against her for a moment before hanging it in the wardrobe, along with John's neatly pressed trousers and shirt. Her concern for Harry far outweighed the excitement she had experienced only hours before, and she bit her lip.

There would be no New Year's celebrations for the family this year.

Hours later, the farm truck drew to a halt outside and Dawn allowed herself to relax. She met John at the gate. The adrenaline that had buzzed through her veins dissipated as he wrapped her in his arms and as they walked through the back door, the lounge clock chimed twelve.

"Happy New Year." Dawn tilted her head back and met his eyes as she manufactured a weak smile. He sighed quietly and attempted a grin before resting his head on her shoulder.

Sleep evaded them both, in spite of their physical exhaustion. It was the wee hours of the morning before Dawn managed to relax in John's arms and drift into a fitful semi-conscious state.

———

Days later, after gruelling rounds of tests, exercises, and examinations, Harry sat propped up in the hospital bed, his face alight with happiness as Dawn bent over to kiss his slightly lop-sided cheek.

"These flowers are from Ed. He said he'll come and see you as soon as you're home," she said.

Harry nodded, lifting his right hand to touch the lemon-coloured lupin in the centre of the bunch before allowing his fingers to trail over the delicate petals of the apricot roses, and the vibrant yellow gerberas. "Thanks."

Alice hastily wiped the drops of saliva from the corner of his mouth with a handkerchief. His face tightened at Alice's touch and Dawn's chest ached with sympathy and embarrassment for him. Succumbing to any weakness, even if it was out of his control, would be difficult for this kind, hardworking farmer.

"He's doing very well," Alice said brightly. "He's been a bit sleepy but the doctors say he's recovering power in his limbs and should be able to drive again in due course."

Dawn relaxed her shoulders and beamed.

"Hay?" Harry stared at John as he mumbled the word.

"Don't worry about the hay, Dad. I've been giving Dawn lessons on both the truck and the tractor, and we'll manage. Anyway, it's right for the moment—probably needs another couple of weeks to ripen properly, and by then you'll be home again and able to supervise."

Harry attempted a grin and Dawn dropped her gaze to the floor. Focusing on Alice's leather shod feet, a frown formed on her forehead. "Alice, your ankles are swollen."

As quick as a wink, Alice tucked her feet under the chair and flapped her hand toward Dawn. "Don't worry about that. I've spent a lot of time sitting around, and my legs are not used to it." She chuckled and diverted Dawn's attention back to Harry. "The doctors said that as soon as he can walk with the stick, and they're happy with his blood pressure, they'll let him come home."

Dawn pretended to take the bait and gazed around the room at the other patients. Four out of the other five residents in the ward were either fast asleep—or unconscious? Dismissing the possibility, Dawn's concern grew as she cast a furtive peep at Alice again, noting the grey tinge to her normally pink cheeks. Alice's slim ankles, rising to shapely calves, were the envy of many women in the district, including Dawn, and as she pulled a chair closer to her mother-in-law, she stretched out her own long, skinny limbs for a subtle comparison. *Perhaps when Harry is well again, we should suggest she has a proper check-up? Lord knows when she last gave herself much consideration.*

The journey home was slow and laborious. Waiting for the signal to move forward at the fourth roadworks site, John tapped his fingers on the steering wheel in time with the radio.

"I think the stress of your Dad's illness is taking its toll on Alice," Dawn said.

John swung a surprised gaze toward Dawn and blinked. "What makes you say that?"

"Didn't you notice how pale she was? And her ankles were swollen."

John shrugged. "I suppose I was concentrating on Dad." The signalman flipped his sign from stop to go and they followed the car in front, carefully negotiating the fine gravel and new tar seal that threatened to splash the lower portions of the vehicle. "It looks like it'll be a while before he's back at the helm."

The anxious edge to his voice sent a spear of concern through Dawn. Like Harry, John was easy-going—at times, frustratingly so. He never wore a watch, preferring to be guided by the sun, the weather, and his stomach. For the first time, an awareness of how vulnerable his good nature made him hit her. *He needs me.* She straightened and took a deep breath.

"I've never been through a hay-making season without his help and direction." John's voice was low, as if this revelation shocked him.

"You've got me. I'm getting better at driving and am quite capable of taking care of your parents' house and animals until they get home."

John reached out and squeezed her hand, shooting her a wide smile. "Thank heaven I've got you. I love you, Dawnie. I sometimes forget to tell you that, don't I? But I do."

She gently rubbed his rough, weather-beaten skin with her thumb. "You don't have to tell me—I know, and I love you too. But … it's nice to hear it all the same."

They continued in silence for a few minutes while Dawn convinced herself that the farm machinery no longer terrified her. Her lack of knowledge, of under-standing, and the pure selfishness she had exhibited in the first year of living on the farm, still made her stomach flip with remorse. *Thank goodness I'm capable of being the strong one now.*

———

DAWN CLUTCHED THE WHEEL, HER HEAD BOBBING AS SHE swivelled her gaze between the side mirror and the haphazard row of tightly pressed squares of hay strewn over the paddock. The loader rattled, its chains rotating noisily until the prongs gripped the end of the bale and the honey-coloured rectangle of precious winter feed progressed up the conveyor belt. Gloved hands, attached to the wiry bodies of Tim or Mike—neither of whom she could see—snatched the twine that bound the package, removed it from the platform, and stacked it on the ever growing jigsaw puzzle of bales on the back of the truck. While Dawn concentrated on nudging the next bale with the guide wings, aligning it perfectly for its ride up the loader, she was only vaguely aware of the men standing high above her. There was no noise except for the machines as all the workers fell into a rhythmic stride, swing, stack, and repeat.

"Whoa!" A bang on the cab roof accompanied the shout and she braked hard. "We're full up. Time to unload."

She released her grip and blew out a long breath, shuffling onto the passenger seat while she waited. It took less than a minute for the men to disconnect the hay elevator and, while Tim jumped into the driver's seat, Mike swung from the running board, leaping off to open the gate and hayshed doors.

"You're doing a great job. Haven't tossed us off once," Tim said as he shifted gears.

Dawn chuckled at Tim's retort and gave him a gentle shove. "I did my best."

John arrived seconds later, and Dawn cast her eyes over the paddock. The tractor and baler stood idle beside the fence, and relief coursed through her. Tomorrow Harry and Alice would be home, and the sight of a neatly mown paddock and a full hay shed would give them both a lift.

She spread the rug on the grass in the shade of the shed and unpacked the box of drinks and sandwiches.

Collapsing in a heap, Tim stretched out his legs, lying back with his hands under his head. "I'm not as fit as I used to be. Perhaps I'm getting too old."

Mike laughed and reached for the mug of cordial Dawn passed him. "I'm a good bit older than you, softy. Too much lying about on the beach I reckon."

"How are Jill and the children enjoying their holiday?" Dawn gulped her drink while she waited for Tim to answer.

"You know kids. They're having a ball. Jill's read a pile of books, and swans around the caravan park chatting to the other holiday-makers. The boys have made a heap of friends so there are no complaints from anyone."

Dawn smiled at the vision. Tim had taken their caravan to Orewa Beach between Christmas and New Year with the intention of joining the family for a much-needed holiday. However, with Harry's unexpected health issues, his intended break had been reduced to a few days.

Marvelling at the cooperation and empathy the Simpson family displayed, her gratitude to her larrikin brother-in-law grew. Without Tim, getting the hay in would have been an exhausting nightmare.

"I'm glad you were able to give us a hand, Mike. Thanks," John said, and Dawn followed her husband's grateful grin to the big man. Dawn was both impressed and relieved that at times like this, their reliable farm scheme man was only a phone call away.

———

SOON AFTER THE SCHOOL HOLIDAYS ENDED, LILLIAN surprised Dawn with the news that she was coming to stay again. "I'm retired now so I can please myself when I want to get away. I shall arrive on the two o'clock train on Friday."

Dawn grinned into the phone. *My, how times change.* "Wonderful, Mum. I'll pick you up from the station."

Leaving home immediately after lunch, Dawn allocated herself just enough time to complete the essential purchases before heading for the hardware shop, followed by the draper's. It was time to freshen up the kitchen walls and having her mother run up new curtains would be a perfect way of keeping her occupied—at least for a couple of hours anyway.

Loaded with her parcel of fabric and carrying a large tin of paint, Dawn glanced down as she stepped from the store, almost crashing into the thin, drab woman on the footpath.

"Oh, I'm sorry. I wasn't looking where I was going," Dawn apologised.

"Dawn. How are you?"

Dawn stared into Carol's heavily lidded eyes, half hidden behind a fall of lank, fair hair, and tried to hide her surprise. "I'm fine. How are you? It's been ages since we caught up." Her gaze dropped to Carol's hand as it rested on her swollen stomach. "Are you …?"

"Yes, I'm pregnant." Carol grimaced, and Dawn raised an eyebrow.

"Congratulations. When is the baby due?"

"Um. In the middle of winter—July, the doctor reckons."

"I'm delighted for you. Would you like to call in for a cuppa sometime? I could trim your hair for you."

Carol shook her head, and Dawn was sure her lip quivered. "I can't. Ron doesn't like me going anywhere without him."

Dawn glanced up and down the street. "Is he with you today?"

"Yes. No. H-he had to deliver a load of calves to the yards. He dropped me off to see the doctor and is picking me up from the grocer's." She swung her gaze up and down the road as she talked, fidgeting with the collar of her dress.

Jealous mongrel. Dawn plastered a smile on her face while her heart went out to the woman.

"Well, if you change your mind, I'd love to have a proper catch-up," Dawn said. Carol's smile was fleeting and Dawn hesitated. "I'm sorry; I have to go too. My mother's coming to stay for a few days and her train will be arriving any tick of the clock."

"Bye, then," Carol said.

As Carol trudged down the path, Dawn remembered her grandmother's words from long ago. *"All choices have consequences. It's how you deal with them that counts."*

As a child, Dawn had had no idea what her gran was talking about. Now she did. The heaviness in her stomach sank deeper while the inability to help made her insides roil.

CHAPTER 22

As summer faded to autumn, Harry's strength increased, his speech became clearer, and although he needed a walking stick to help him move about the house, he was able to return to riding Rambler. He reasoned that he could put his trust in the old gelding, and the horse would be capable of making decisions that a vehicle could not.

Hoover appeared delighted to have his master home and overnight, seemed to morph from a hyperactive and enthusiastic dog that sometimes bordered on disobedient to displaying the temperament of a quiet thinker. He only had to look at Harry in order to know exactly what was required of him.

While the family adjusted to the new, more measured way of life, Lillian developed the habit of catching the train to Helensville every few weeks, staying several days on each occasion before requesting

Dawn drive her back to town. Slowly but surely, their relationship improved, and Dawn prayed it would continue. While still getting used to the 'new mum', she relished the opportunities to ask questions about her father and extended family, and her hopes crashed again at the discovery that the few connections she may have had were now long gone. She clung to the belief that the friendship between mother and daughter would evolve and maybe, just maybe, one day she and John would be blessed with a child they could all dote on. It was a topic no longer discussed, but deep in her heart, Dawn clung to the facts. She was still young and healthy and achieving a pregnancy did not appear to be impossible. Seeing it through was the hard part.

On the first Saturday in May, excitement built in the community as the duck shooting season began with the annual ritual of friends and relatives keen to take part, gathering together. Every pond, lake, swamp, or river in the district would be under close scrutiny for the following three weeks. Dawn had been mortified when John had explained that the season had originally been introduced for both food and to control the increasing population of wild ducks. She was deeply grateful when the Simpson family made the decision to no longer allow shooters on their land. With the setting of the sun, the sound of gunfire faded and the family gathered at Alice and Harry's for the Sunday evening meal.

Once again, Lillian had taken up temporary residence in the spare room at Dawn and John's, delighted to have timed her stay with Ed and Hilde's monthly visit to the Fantail Ridge homestead.

Dawn bit her lip, stifling a grin as her mother engaged the big Norwegian in conversation, seemingly enthralled at the knowledge he shared about bird life on the peninsula. Ed had not changed physically in the few years Dawn had known him, however, since Hilde's arrival, a softer, more social man had evolved. On the other hand, Hilde appeared thinner, more tired and … much older than her brother. Dawn dismissed the elderly woman's lack of interaction, knowing how deaf she had become, and instead, cleared the plates and rested her hand on Hilde's. "Would you like some dessert? I've made a lemon meringue pie."

Hilde's long, narrow face lit up. "Thank you. I would."

While Dawn carried the dessert and stack of bowls to the table, Alice rose to remove the tray of homemade ice cream from the freezer. Dawn returned to the kitchen to collect the serving utensils, and as she reached for the cake trowel, the knife slipped from her hand and crashed to the floor.

"Oh, bother!" She bent and picked it up, sucking in a sharp intake of breath as her eyes rested on Alice's ankles. Her feet were puffy and the swelling rose up her legs, almost to her calves.

"Alice," Dawn whispered as she nudged her mother-in-law. "Your feet are awfully swollen. Let me do that. You sit down."

"Don't worry about me, love. I've probably been trying to do a bit much, what with Harry and all that." Her voice dropped to barely a whisper too, and Dawn had to lean forward to hear her. "Don't say anything to Harry. I don't want to worry him. I'm fine."

Dawn frowned, deciding that Alice's words proved otherwise. She would need both Harry and John to help her get this stoic, independent woman to town for a medical check.

With dinner over, everyone moved into the sitting room, relaxing with their cups of tea and watching the news on television when the phone rang.

"I'll get it." John headed to the hallway alcove.

He closed the door behind him, and Dawn barely heard the murmurings as she concentrated on Harry's plan for the upcoming shearing.

The door flew open. Dawn gasped as John stared at his family, his eyes wide, rubbing his chin.

"That was Clive. Apparently, Ron Woods didn't go home after today's shoot and no one seems to know where he is."

"Do you … um, is it possible he's had a bit much to drink and is sleeping it off somewhere?" Harry asked.

Ed's forehead creased and his eyes narrowed. He

shook his head. "No. That man always makes it home, no matter how much he drinks."

Dawn studied Ed, surprised at the revelation. *I didn't realise you knew him so well, although you're close to Carol so it probably makes sense?*

"What does Clive suggest?" Harry had moved to the edge of his chair, his hand resting on the top of his walking stick.

"There's not much we can do until it's been established exactly where he was shooting. Apparently, he went to the lake near the forestry with a few mates. They had two boats and at least one hide and had arranged to meet back at the vehicles at seven o'clock. Everyone else returned on time but not Ron. One of the boats is missing. They've called the police and they're on their way out. I suppose there will be a few questions to answer before they decide on a plan."

The relaxed feel in the room faltered. The fire flickered, and a shiver ran down Dawn's spine. She leaned forward and poked the embers, dropping another piece of wood in the grate. She had only seen Ron at a distance and had never spoken to him. However, her encounters with Carol and the deep-seated concern she had for her wellbeing set her alarm bells ringing.

"John, I think perhaps we should go home now." Ed stood, staring contemplatively around the group. "A search party may be required, and I would like to be included."

"Of course. We'll drop Dawn and Lillian at home on

our way, and I'll collect my spotlight and backpack just in case," John replied.

Empty cups clattered into saucers as everyone stood and gathered their belongings.

"See you in the morning." Dawn hugged Alice before slipping her arms into her jacket. "Thanks for the lovely dinner. I'll collect the pudding dish tomorrow."

Squeezing into the middle of the back seat, Dawn waved through the front windscreen to Harry and Alice, standing arm in arm at the gate.

John closed Hilde's door before sliding behind the steering wheel. "They're worried. They've lived here for so long and are the backbone of this community. When anything is amiss, you've always been able to count on them to help. Now, with Dad not being as well as he wants to be, he'll be feeling anxious and useless."

"Well, let's hope the silly man turns up by the time you get to Ed and Hilde's and everyone can get a good night's sleep." Lillian sniffed her disapproval and stared through the side window as Dawn's concern grew.

DAWN WOKE WITH A JOLT. HOW LONG HAD SHE SLEPT? With eyes wide open, she strained her ears. A light flicked on and her pulse slowed as John's familiar footfalls echoed softly in the hallway.

"Did you find him?" she asked as he came into their room.

"No, but the second boat was located—empty. We covered as much ground as we could. The police were worried someone would trip over in the dark and end up getting hurt. They've called off the search until daylight tomorrow. Ed said he'll milk earlier than usual and I'll pick him up at half past seven."

Dawn yawned and snuggled under the eiderdown. "What's the time?"

"Half past one. It'll be a short night, so we'd better make the most of it."

Within a minute, Dawn registered his regular, gentle breathing and allowed herself to drop off to sleep.

———

IT TOOK TWO DAYS OF EXHAUSTIVE SEARCHING BEFORE Ron's body was dragged from the depths of the lake, bloated and entangled with reeds.

John slept for almost twelve hours before he appeared in the doorway, tousled, and wearing pyjamas.

"Planting bulbs?"

Dawn dropped her trowel and strode across the lawn to give him a hug. "Yes. I had to do something useful to pass the time until you woke." She craned her neck around the side of the house and called, "John's awake, Mum. We're going inside for a cuppa."

Lillian appeared from behind the front garden bed with a bunch of roses in one hand and a pair of secateurs in the other. "Lovely. I'll pop these in a vase and join you in a minute."

Minutes later, Dawn poured the tea and pushed a plate of toast slathered with home-made strawberry jam into the middle of the table before taking a seat opposite her mother. She studied John's worried face.

"How did the accident happen?" Dawn spoke softly, her forehead creased. "From the little I've heard, he's been a keen and successful shooter every year, in spite of his failings."

John cleared his throat, rubbing a hand over his whiskery chin as he switched the kettle on. "The police are questioning everyone and the coroner will be involved, so I suppose we'll find out in due course."

"But …? You think there's more to it?"

"Well, no. Not necessarily. I heard a few of the search party talking, that's all. Some wonder if he committed suicide. Others are questioning foul play."

Dawn sat back in her chair, her mouth open. "Really? Out here in quiet little South Head? No. He may not have been very pleasant but …"

John shook his head and poured the tea. "Give it time."

Dawn rested her elbows on the table, leaning forward with her chin in her hands. *Poor Carol. How must she be feeling?* "Their baby is due in a couple of months. I hope Carol will be alright."

John put the teapot down, his eyes meeting Dawn's in a long, measured stare. "I wouldn't be surprised if she's more than alright. I'm aware that you know her better than I do, but I reckon she's better off without him."

"She might not feel that way if she loves him. Anyway, however she feels, I'm sure she will be in shock."

Dawn's thoughts dwelled on the thin, timid woman she had bumped into in the main street only a week or two ago. Carol had a habit of looking over her shoulder every few minutes, as though frightened of something, or someone. Dawn heaved a sigh. She could only assume that John was right. The poor woman would very likely be better off without him.

"Whatever happens, I want to go to the funeral. I suspect Carol will need every friend she can find."

CHAPTER 23

It was almost two weeks before Ron's body was released and the funeral could proceed.

Dawn gazed around the small crowd inside the church, nodding politely to familiar faces and surprised by the number of neighbours attending. *I suppose they want to pay their respects to Carol, just as we do.* The front pew on one side of the aisle held only Carol and the elderly couple that Dawn remembered from the first New Year's Eve dance. Carol's head was bowed, her shoulders slumped in a dark green coat that had clearly seen better days. Across from her, three burly men in black suits sat shoulder to shoulder, their backs to the congregation.

Dawn turned as the door was closed, shutting out the cold wind that blew from the south. The local police sergeant perched on the end of the last pew and Dawn shuffled in her seat as John whispered, "Those blokes up the front were involved in the search. Apparently they're Ron's shooting mates."

Dawn studied their unfamiliar profiles again as the minister emerged from the vestry, stood at the altar, and raised his hands.

———

STANDING OUTSIDE THE CHURCH ALMOST AN HOUR later, Dawn waited until the Hearse drove away and then moved toward Carol. Carol was flanked by the older couple on one side and an unfamiliar woman on the other. Dawn hesitated, waiting her turn to share her condolences. The police sergeant bent to speak to the woman, and a man bearing a large bunch of flowers stopped in front of the elderly couple, gesturing toward the cars as if asking where he should take them.

Dawn moved in front of Carol and reached out, enveloping her in a hug. "I'm so sorry for your loss. I hope you and the baby will be alright?"

Clinging to Dawn as though she were sinking, Carol turned her head slightly and whispered in her Dawn's ear.

"No loss." She released her and smiled wanly.

Dawn flinched at her words, uncertain if she had heard correctly. She returned the quick smile, momentarily frozen to the spot. Had she imagined it? Did Carol just wink?

Perhaps the wind blew something into her eye. Yes, that was what happened.

John appeared at her shoulder and reached for Carol's hand. "I'm very sorry, Carol. Please accept our condolences and our early departure. We've got the shearers coming tomorrow."

"Thank you for coming." Carol turned to greet approaching mourners and Dawn stepped aside. Clinging to John as they left the church yard, she walked blindly to the car, her thoughts a tangled web.

Long after John fell asleep that night, Dawn's eyes remained wide open and her body, stiff, as she replayed Carol's words over and over again.

Ron's life had been a mystery to most residents in the district—would his death be the same? The coroner's court had ruled it an accidental drowning, but … Dawn wasn't so sure.

———

SINCE HARRY'S STROKE, DAWN FOUND HERSELF spending more time on the farm helping John, and not only during the frantic periods of hay-making, shearing, crutching, and weaning. With the exception of the boring role as chief fencing assistant, where she discovered passing battens and staples to John was as repetitious and tedious as watching paint dry, she found herself enjoying her new busyness. With her days filled to overflowing from early morning bird call until dark, she barely had time to dwell on any more than the job at hand and accepted that this year was proving to be more frantic than usual.

Her fear of horses had waned slightly, but not enough to want to learn to ride. Dawn walked behind the sheep with the dogs, allowing Gyp to remain at her side while Sandy and Hoover ran back and forth, keeping the flock together. It didn't take long for her to realise that the dogs did all the work, and if they could have opened the gates, she was sure they would have managed perfectly well without her. Nevertheless, her confidence and knowledge grew with every passing day.

The weather broke days later and blustery showers swept off the Tasman, rattling the windows and forcing the freshly shorn sheep to form huddles under trees and against the thick, native bush.

Bales of wool filled one end of the shed and Harry busied himself in the office, catching up on paperwork. John had disappeared to work on machinery that was showing signs of stress, and Dawn folded the final pile of clean washing and looked around her orderly house, wondering what to do next.

In the laundry, a bucket of water sat in the tub, overflowing with flowers that Dawn had picked the previous day. Winter was coming and it would be slim pickings for a couple of months—and she hadn't wanted them bashed to bits by the predicted weather front. As they caught her eye, her plans to fill the vases changed. She lifted them, dripping water and leaves on the floor, then laid them on a thick wad of newspaper and trimmed the stems. Then, wrapping them carefully in a fresh piece of paper, she tied the bundle with a piece of string and laid them on an old towel.

Minutes later, she had exchanged her farm clothes for warm slacks and a jersey and was driving across the paddock.

Hesitating in front of a solid gate, its bottom rail half buried in mud and with one hinge hanging, she pulled the handbrake on and climbed out of the car. Her heart thumped. The austere entrance discouraged entry to all but the bravest soul, and she swallowed hard. Should she or shouldn't she?

Drawing her shoulders back, she clamped her lips together and unlatched the gate, dragging it across the track as she picked her way carefully through the mud.

In spite of overgrown weeds and thistles throughout the house paddock, the porch of the shabby old house was swept clean. A pair of gumboots stood against the wall beneath an oilskin coat.

She lifted her hand to knock and jumped back as the door opened.

Dawn stuttered. "H-hello." She handed the bunch of flowers to Carol.

"Hi. Do you want to come in?" Carol took the bouquet and stepped back, ushering Dawn inside.

In spite of her advanced pregnancy, Dawn noted a lightness in Carol's step, her clean, shiny hair, and a confidence she that had clearly evaded her in the years since they'd met.

Dawn's astonishment increased as she followed Carol into the kitchen. Contrary to the neglected appearance of both the farm and house, it was clear Carol was no slouch. With the exception of a row of packing boxes against the wall, inside, the shabby walls and surfaces were spotless and the worn linoleum on the floor shone.

"Are you moving?" Dawn inclined her head toward the boxes while Carol removed a jug from a cupboard and unwrapped the flowers.

"Yes. I have to." There was no sign of sorrow or apology in her statement. "It seems that the bank owns the majority of this place and Ron's conniving brother owns the balance." She shrugged and placed the flowers on the table.

Dawn's eyes widened in disgust. "Where are you going? Will you be alright?"

Carol snorted. "I'll be a darn sight better off than I've been these past few years … I'm going home."

Dawn blinked hard, astonished at Carol's decisive tone. The timid, mouse-like girl had disappeared and in her place was a determined, positive woman.

"Sit down. I'll make a cup of tea."

Dawn moved to the table and pulled out a chair. As she brushed against the wall, she accidentally bumped the calendar hanging immediately next to her, and it swung wildly on its hook. Her eyes widened as she glimpsed a gaping hole behind it, and she silently met Carol's gaze.

"Yes, I'm sure you know this was never a happy home. I'm grateful to be the one still alive—and to have my baby to look forward to." Carol placed a mug of tea in front of her and sat down. "My parents live in Hamilton, and I'm going to move in with them. They're getting old now and are looking forward to having us both for company." She rubbed her stomach as her tone softened.

"Were they the people with you at the funeral?"

"Yes. They took me in when I was four. My mother died of a drug overdose, and I have no idea who my father was." She shrugged and grinned at Dawn. "Don't look so shocked. There's a big world out there that well-brought-up girls like you know nothing about."

Dawn clamped her teeth together and wrapped her hands around her mug. It was true. Her strained relationship with her mother and deceased father may not have been ideal, but she'd had a comfortable home with a warm fire in the winter and a well-supported education. She swallowed a mouthful of tea as discomfort squirmed within her.

"Would you like to keep in touch?" Dawn stared at Carol, stiff and expecting rejection.

A wide smile spread across Carol's face, and she reached across the table and squeezed Dawn's hand. "Actually, I'd like that. Perhaps we could exchange Christmas cards. I'm not one for writing much, but I'll keep in contact with Ed and Hilde and I'll ask them to share my letters with you. Will that do?"

Dawn laughed. "It certainly will. I'm a hopeless correspondent too but I'd love to hear about your baby when it arrives—and I know Ed and Hilde would be devastated if you lost contact with them."

"Deal." Carol reached for the teapot and held it aloft. "More?"

Dawn glanced through the window, surprised to see how far the sun had slid toward the horizon. "No, thank you. I'd better get home. I didn't realise how late it was."

The women walked outside together and hugged briefly before Dawn slid into her car.

"I'll do the gate." Carol grinned. "There's a knack to getting it closed while keeping your feet clean and dry."

Dawn waved out the window, gripping the steering wheel with one hand as she turned for home. Sadness wove inside her, an emptiness that she couldn't explain. *She's a tough woman. Tougher than me anyway.*

Her admiration for Carol was tinged with selfishness. Their friendship would never have been the same as the one she shared with Ann—but in spite of their brief acquaintance, she was disappointed that Carol was moving away.

CHAPTER 24

Winter, 1972

The seasons rolled from summer to a brief spell of autumn before an early cold and wet winter set in. On one of the rare days filled with sunshine and a soft breeze when Harry phoned.

"Would you mind giving us a hand drafting the weaner calves? Alice is a bit tired today, and I'd like to get over to the run-off and take them off their mothers before they outgrow the poor old girls."

"Sure. I'd love to help." Dawn was pleasantly surprised at Harry's request. Although Alice had finally relented and visited the doctor, her condition appeared to be deteriorating and Dawn was concerned. With their usual GP on holidays during her previous check-up, had the young relieving locum doctor missed something?

"Righto. We'll get the job done before this darned

weather breaks again. John will be on the horse and I'll do my best but I'm not quite as quick as I once was. Perhaps you could manage the gate that Alice usually operates."

Dawn agreed and her heart gave a skip. She had joined in on many a muster, however she was more of a spectator than a participant, sitting on the fence while the men moved carefully around the herd and Alice worked the drafting gate. They called her the 'spotter'—the one who could see from above, alerting those in the yards of anything that may put them in danger.

This year, things were more serious. Harry's forehead wore a permanent network of worry lines, and his limp seemed more pronounced than in recent weeks. Alice spent less time helping on the farm, resting every afternoon in order to cope with the evening chores, and Dawn was grateful that at last, she was not only needed, but she was also a useful and necessary part of the Simpson team.

The sunshine hadn't lasted and after lunch, John closed the newspaper and heaved a sigh. He got to his feet and stared through the window as rain slashed the glass pane.

"Looks like fuel prices are going up again. This war between Israel and the Middle East is going to affect us big time."

"Can we do anything to ease it?" Dawn threw

another log on the fire and plonked herself on the rug by the hearth.

"We can't help with the fuel prices—that's well and truly out of our control. I suppose we'll have to adjust our budget again. Reduce the amount of petrol we use and hope it's short-lived."

Dawn frowned. This was not the John she knew. *Should I be worried?* She plastered a smile on her face and crossed the room to hug him. "In that case, I suppose all we can do is continue farming to the best of our ability—and hope for the best?

———

COWS BELLOWED AND PAWED THE GROUND AS JOHN ushered them into the smaller pen, waving his hat in their faces. Honey, his horse, swung back and forth on her hindquarters, her tail swishing as she plunged boldly between the cow and calf. Almost as big as their mothers now, the calves were three times the size of the gentle dairy breeds and Dawn had a healthy respect for them.

"Are you right, love?" John's gaze didn't leave the cattle as he called. "I'll push the first one up now. Just slam that sliding gate the second its backside passes you. Okay?"

Dawn had watched Alice on many occasions and was sure it couldn't be too hard.

As the first skittish youngster raced into the crush,

she shoved with all her might and the gate clanged shut, locking the beast in the small, concrete-floored section of the yard. Harry moved forward, closing the head bail behind the calf's ears, talking quietly to the animal as he slid the needle into its neck, squeezed the syringe, and quickly inspected its eyes. Within seconds, the health check was completed, the head bail released, and the calf rushed forward into the other end of the yard, all on its lonesome. The process was repeated until, under much protesting from their mothers, there were no youngsters left to check, and Dawn could return to the truck to collect the thermos flasks and sandwiches.

Replenished by lunch, John and the dogs herded the calves toward a fresh paddock that was untouched since the previous year, keeping them together in a tight mob and putting several strong fences between the weaners and their mothers. Dawn spread bales of hay around the outside perimeter of the yards, then jerked to a stop. Although winter wasn't yet over, a tiny lupin flower had poked its head through the damp earth, and she beamed. It didn't matter how often she came to the run-off, or what season it was—she was always looking for the colourful spires, hoping she would find one. As the grass thickened and cattle trampled the ground, the display of lupins had reduced a little more each year, but to her, even small patches of flowers were enough to lift the spirits and provide new hope and inspiration.

The temperature dropped and a wild squall blew in from the Tasman as she and Harry drove home. Dawn wound the truck window up tightly and huddled against her seat.

"I reckon you might be running a hot bath for John when we get home. He'll be frozen stiff in this." Harry's frown deepened farther, and Dawn chewed her lip.

"I hope the weaners won't be too miserable."

Harry chuckled. "Don't you worry about them. You saw how big they are—and how their mothers were more interested in the hay than their babies. At least now they can have a rest for a few weeks before they calve again."

Dawn squirmed. Poor cows. She wasn't sure which was worse—having a baby every year of your fertile life, or never having a baby at all.

Dawn's concern grew for Alice the following evening when she and John joined his parents for dinner. Alice's sheepskin slippers didn't quite hide the swelling around her ankles and, instead of protesting when Dawn told her to watch television while she and John did the dishes, she obeyed, seemingly grateful to collapse onto the couch and put her feet up.

"We should take her to the doctor." Dawn kept her voice low as she bent over the sudsy water.

John remained mute, and she stopped scrubbing

and looked into his eyes. Sadness lengthened his face and he drew a long, slow breath. "I don't know. I can't bear to think of my parents getting old and ill."

"We're all going to get old, love. It's the ill bit that I'm worried about right now." She returned her attention to the sink while a plan formed. Taking time to wring out the dishcloth first, she wiped the benches and stovetop before speaking. "I'm going to town later this week to do some shopping and was planning to call in on Jill at the same time. Perhaps your mum will come with me for an outing."

John's easy smile returned when they asked Alice a few minutes later and she grinned.

"I'd love to come. I'm afraid I really don't enjoy driving as much as I used to. There are too many cars now, and I can't have the road to myself," Alice said.

Laughter split the air and Harry tsk-tsked. "You're not supposed to have the road to yourself. You're supposed to keep to the left-hand side, even if you are on gravel and there's no stripe down the middle to guide you."

Dawn chuckled again, pleased she had suggested she drive now that she knew Alice's attitude.

"I might pop into the chemist and see if he can give me something for this blimming indigestion while we're in town." Alice returned her attention to the television, seemingly unaware of the horrified expressions that both John and Dawn exchanged.

"HI JILL." DAWN GAVE HER SISTER-IN-LAW A CHEERY wave as she hurried to the passenger side and held the door open for Alice.

"I've got the kettle on. Perfect timing because I've even baked a fresh batch of scones."

"I think this was a good suggestion of yours, Dawn." Alice smiled at both women as she clutched the handrail and took the three steps slowly, treading each one with both feet before continuing to the next.

Jill narrowed her eyes, meeting Dawn's concerned glance as Alice stepped through the doorway. Dawn was pleased she had phoned the previous night, warning Jill of Alice's declining health and discussing the best way of convincing her she needed a check-up.

"It's quiet without the boys, isn't it?" Alice glanced down the hallway as she spoke as if expecting the thunder of children's footsteps to disturb the peace.

"It certainly is—and I am very grateful for the few hours I get each day to catch up around here." Jill grinned as she placed the teapot and plate of scones on the table.

Although the house was never quite as pristine as her own, Dawn couldn't help but notice the improvements Jill had made since Richard had started school. The living area and kitchen had been painted and the worktops rarely held more than a bowl of fruit and electric kettle—a far cry from the clutter she had encountered on her first visit. Overflowing baskets of washing waiting to be folded still managed to present themselves from time to time, but one look at the healthy abundance of flowers and shrubs outside more than explained Jill's time priorities.

Dawn reached for a scone and lathered it with butter and jam.

"I thought we might all go into town together. Is that okay with you, Dawn?" Jill asked.

"Of course. We haven't done that for such a long time, this could be fun."

"Lunch will be my treat—we'll do our shopping and go to the Why Not tea room once we've finished." Alice lifted the dainty china cup to her lips before patting her mouth with the serviette. "Thank you, Jill. That was lovely."

Dawn pushed her chair back and gathered the empty cups. "Come on then, ladies. Let's begin."

CHAPTER 25

Dawn was not been surprised when the chemist had refused to supply Alice with indigestion medication over the counter.

"You need to see the doctor first as it could be caused by many things. When was the last time you had a proper examination?"

Alice frowned and stared at Dawn, as though hoping she could pluck a date out of thin air. "I can't remember."

"You haven't since I've been in the family anyway—and that's nearly seven years." Dawn spoke quietly.

The chemist nodded seriously and escorted them to the door. "Please go and make an appointment straight away."

Stopping at the grocery store first, Dawn whispered to Jill while Alice was chatting with the girl at the counter. "I'll go and get the car. I know it's not far to the doctor's surgery but it's uphill all the way, and from the look on the chemist's face when he saw Alice's swollen ankles, I don't think she should walk."

Jill nodded and moved closer to Alice as Dawn slipped outside.

While Dawn and Jill sat in the waiting room, the nurse taking Alice's blood pressure was just visible through the gap in the partially closed door. The doctor appeared briefly from a side room, dropping a folder at the reception desk before entering the one containing Alice. He closed the door firmly behind him.

They waited for more than half an hour before the door opened again and the doctor beckoned the two of them inside. Alice lay on the examination bed, her face as pale as the pillowcase and Dawn reached out and clasped her hand.

"I'm afraid Mrs Simpson is not at all well. I'm sending her to Greenlane Hospital to see a heart specialist as soon as I can get an appointment for her."

"Oh." It took Dawn a few seconds to register the seriousness of the doctor's comments. She shot a glance toward Jill, who was staring open-mouthed at the man—as if he were speaking a foreign language. "When?"

"The receptionist is phoning now and the nurse will help Mrs Simpson dress. Please take a seat while we get things organised." He nodded and gave the two of them a quick smile before returning to the reception area.

"W-what will I tell Harry?" Alice's voice shook and Dawn rested her hand gently on Alice's.

"Don't worry. You have been so stoic and strong for Harry. You know he will be the same for you. Anyway, I'm sure this is just a temporary setback—and a good thing that we came today." Dawn shot Alice a reassuring smile as she spoke.

Jill gave Alice a hug, remaining mute and calm.

"Here you are." The nurse bustled into the room and handed a sheet of paper to Alice, her smile bright and encouraging. "Let's get you up now. I'll help you put your shoes on so you don't have to bend."

While assisting Alice, the bubbly nurse continued. "We've managed to get you an appointment with the specialist on Wednesday morning at half past nine. I suggest you pack a bag in case he wants you to stay a couple of days while he runs tests."

Alice's hand flew to her chest and her voice wobbled. "Oh my goodness. This all sounds a bit serious."

"You'll be well looked after, Mrs Simpson. At least we'll all know what we're dealing with by the end of the week." The nurse patted Alice's hand and let them out to the reception area.

Today's Monday. Dawn's mind raced. *Should John or I take both his parents to the hospital? How can we juggle this and take care of the farm at the same time?*

"Come on. Let's get back to my place and have a cup of tea. I'll ring Susan and see if she's free to take you to the appointment." Jill rose to her feet and tucked her arm into Alice's elbow, steadying her as she stood.

"Great idea." Dawn drew a long breath and swallowed her fears. "Susan is used to driving around in the city. Perhaps you and Harry could go to their place tomorrow afternoon before peak-hour traffic starts, then you'll be nice and handy for Wednesday."

———

As they stood by the gate outside the homestead the following day, Dawn held John's hand tightly, rubbing his arm in an effort to soften the hard line of his jaw.

"She'll be fine, sweetheart." She waved at the departing vehicle, Alice's neatly permed white hair and Harry's going-to-town hat imprinted on her mind as the car descended the hill. A knot had formed in her stomach, and she crossed her fingers behind her back. During the past few years, Alice had been her greatest teacher, mentor, and friend. Her memories fled to the outspoken, and unappreciative young woman who had joined the Simpson family in spring of 1966. Those days were long gone, and now, with John's love and support, she was determined to make it up to Alice and Harry.

The next twenty-four hours dragged, and neither Dawn nor John could find the energy to complete anything but the essential chores. When the phone eventually rang late on Wednesday afternoon, they both sprang to answer it, pressing their heads together against the receiver as Susan relayed the news.

"She has a heart condition, which is preventing her blood from pumping correctly and therefore causing fluid build-up in her ankles and feet."

"And the pains in her chest? Are they indigestion?" Dawn's concern had escalated at the mention of Alice's heart.

"No. They're due to a condition called angina—which is also heart-related. Provided Alice takes the prescribed medication, the doctor is quite sure she will be with us for a while yet."

"What drugs will she have to be on?" The creases on John's forehead deepened as he spoke.

"One every day to reduce the fluid and help with circulation, and when she gets a chest pain, she has tiny blue tablets to pop under her tongue. Other than that, we have to ensure she gets plenty of rest."

Dawn let the air whoosh from her lungs as she slithered onto the couch. She hadn't realised how anxious she'd been, and gratefully allowed John to have the receiver to himself while the conversation continued.

"That's great. Thanks, Susan. We'll look forward to seeing them home again on the weekend." He paused and nodded at the phone. "Bye." He dropped the receiver into its holder and collapsed on the sofa next to Dawn.

"Susan suggested Mum and Dad stay with them for a couple more nights. Just to make sure the medication is taking effect, and so she and George can ensure they rest properly."

"I guess this means we really should change a few work responsibilities?"

"Yes. It's great that Dad is more or less back to his old self, but I think we'll try to take over some of the jobs that keep him away from the house for long periods." John squeezed Dawn's hand. "How do you reckon you'll go as my truck driver and off-sider in the shearing shed?"

Dawn grinned and sucked in a deep breath. "Well, I think it's about time. We'll make a good team—just wait and see."

———

THE FOLLOWING THREE DAYS WERE FILLED TO CAPACITY as Jill joined Dawn in giving Alice and Harry's house a spring clean. The curtains and window were washed, the oven cleaned and polished until it sparkled, and every surface dusted.

While the women worked inside, John weeded the gardens and built another large pen near their own cottage that could house orphaned lambs, calves, or other waifs and strays that Alice would frequently care for.

"We shouldn't take the house cow or your Mum's

chooks—and definitely not Major. Your parents will still want to feel needed, and taking every chore from them that had shaped their lives for more than sixty years might not be appreciated."

John rubbed his chin. "Okay, you win. We'll let Dad milk the cow after she's calved and Mum can keep her chooks and fuss over the old horse."

"You're a good man, John Simpson."

———

A WEEK LATER, WITH ALICE AND HARRY ENSCONCED back in the homestead and apparently relieved with the new regime, Dawn received a phone call from Hilde.

"Could you come and get us please? We would like to visit Alice."

"Of course, Hilde. Would tomorrow suit? I am cutting Mrs Radley's hair at ten o'clock so can pop out and get you after I leave her place. Come and have lunch with us all, and I'll make sure we get you home in time for milking."

"Thank you. I shall make something to share for lunch."

"Thanks Hilde. See you in the morning."

Dawn smiled as she hung up the phone. Hilde and Ed had never visited without bringing far more food with them than they ate. The first time they'd brought a box full of vegetables and fish and Dawn had been about to object but caught sight of Alice's headshake just in time. After they had gone home again, Alice had explained. *"They have no family except each other and are very proud people who like to help others. The least we can do is to accept their gifts in the manner they are being given—with sincere appreciation."*

———

THE NEXT DAY, DAWN WENT TO COLLECT ED AND Hilde. Their arrival seemed to spark Alice up, and Dawn was equally delighted when Ed handed her a letter.

"It's from Carol. She asked me to pass on the news, but I'm sure you'd rather read it for yourself."

"Thank you." While the others moved into the living room, Dawn filled the kettle. While she stood waiting for it to boil, she pulled the thin sheets of writing paper from the envelope and read.

Dear Ed, Hilde, and Dawn,

I hope you don't mind sharing this letter. I am quite busy now and very happy. My baby boy was born almost a month ago and I have called him Justin. He is beautiful and a very good baby. I am not sure who he looks like, but he has dark eyes and hair so hasn't taken after either Ron or myself in that area. Mum and Dad are well and are enjoying having us at home with them.

In a little while (perhaps when Justin is able to tolerate solids), I will be starting a part-time job in our local super-

market. Mum and Dad will care for him while I am working and the money will be very welcome for us all.

As we live relatively close to the new public gardens in Hamilton, I am able to take Justin for a long walk each day. The lake and roses are beautiful, and it reminds me of your garden, Ed and Hilde.

I think of you all often and hope you are keeping well.

Love to you all,

Carol and Justin

"How's the tea coming along?"

Dawn jumped as John appeared at her elbow. "Sorry. I was just reading the letter from Carol." She poured the water into the teapot before snatching up a ladle and passing it to John. "You take the soup in and I'll bring the tea?"

While the others ate, Dawn stirred her soup idly and sipped her tea slowly as her mind drifted. She was pleased to hear Carol's news, and even more pleased to know she was safe and happy. It would have been nice to be able to visit her, but with Hamilton three hours' drive away, she doubted the trip was possible—at least in the foreseeable future.

Would their paths ever cross again?

CHAPTER 26

Spring, 1975

It wasn't only the sudden change of temperature that boosted Dawn's mood, but the softening of the breeze, the daffodils, and the new lambs that bounded around the paddocks. As she strode across the fresh young shoots of grass to the mailbox, a strange feeling came over her. It was as though she were drifting, floating above herself, and she stopped, waiting for it to pass. *Am I coming down with something?* She had experienced a similar feeling only a week before. But no, she was quite sure there was nothing wrong—physically, anyway.

The mailbox was overflowing, and she lay the bread on the ground while she organised the pile of newspapers and letters, and a small parcel addressed to Alice. Then, resting the loaf of bread on top of the mail, she ambled back to the house, pausing at the cross under the peach tree where Gyp lay. It had only been two months since she'd died in her sleep, and Dawn wasn't surprised how much she missed the old dog.

Alice and Harry had gone on a holiday, their combined health problems inspiring them to enjoy whatever time they had left. It saddened Dawn that they weren't around as often but they made light of it, laughing and reassuring her that it was time they caught up with distant members of the family before it was too late.

"We want to reinforce the relationships with those closest to us and make amends with those that aren't," Alice had said, chuckling.

In truth, John was convinced that it was something they had wanted to do for a long time but hadn't felt comfortable with until the reins of responsibility for the farm had been removed. After Alice's heart scare, Dawn and John stepped up, and both Harry and Alice finally admitted it was a relief. Dawn wondered now how they had managed to do so much for so long. No wonder they had health issues.

The farm dogs were permanently kennelled near John and Dawn's cottage and the farm deliveries arrived in their mailbox instead of the homestead's.

After sorting the mail into piles and slipping her parents-in-law's personal mail into the folder she kept in the old slimline desk for that purpose, Dawn switched the kettle on and opened the tea caddy. She recoiled as the aroma reached her nose and slammed the lid back on. *What on earth is going on? I've always loved the smell of tea.*

Instead, she pulled out the bottle of Ed's rhubarb cordial from the cupboard and mixed herself a large glassful.

She slumped in the chair and rested her elbows on the table, staring through the window at the nodding heads of jonquils and daffodils that lined the southern garden and overflowed into the paddock.

Frowning, she ran her mind through the list of possibilities. Pregnancy was out of the question—her cycle was still relatively normal—for her, anyway. It had never been that regular but it was still happening. Her previous pregnancies had been obvious from the start and the sickness had confirmed any suspicions she may have had. This time, it had to be something else.

She sat bolt upright as lights flashed for a split second and her head spun. Could it be something more sinister? A sinking feeling drained the last of her energy, and she folded her arms on the table and lay her head on them. *Oh Lord, after the year we've had, the last thing we need is another health scare?*

Ten minutes later, she was back to normal and she mixed the lambs' bottles and zipped up her jacket. John had gone to bring the last of the previous year's drop closer to the yards. The year had been a kind one and last season's lambs had grown quickly, bringing slightly better money than in previous years. They had kept over a hundred, allowing them to mature a little more and cut their first adult teeth, deeming them hoggets instead of lambs. Dawn grinned as she remembered the first year on the farm. When John had asked if she would like to help him with the hoggets, she had been looking around for pigs, puzzled and confused. All she could see were sheep. He had thought it hilarious until she had stormed off in a huff and he'd come running after her, full of apologies and an explanation.

She realised now how her behaviour must have seemed—naive and selfish. It wasn't something she was proud of. Looking around at the neat farm layout, the garden that burst with colour, and the freshly painted white walls of the house brought her pride and satisfaction. She had finally grown up.

When the dizziness returned the following day, she phoned the medical centre and made an appointment, convincing herself it would be an ear infection or something related to the change in weather.

This time, it was she who stared at the doctor in shock.

"Congratulations. You are pregnant."

"Are you sure?" Dawn gaped at the man, heat rising to her face. Her heart gave a little skip, and then the familiar dread sank like a stone within her. "Will I lose this one as well?"

"We hope not, Mrs Simpson. You are already well past the first trimester."

"But how can I be? I'm still getting my monthly cycle—and I'm not sick."

The doctor gave a small smile. "Every mother is different, and every pregnancy takes its own course. It's quite common to continue experiencing some spotting and even light bleeding in the first couple of months. I suggest you go home and take good care of yourself. Rest when you can and avoid lifting anything heavy."

"So … if everything goes well this time, when will the baby be due?"

"I would estimate around late March next year." He scribbled something on the notepaper in front of him. "Come and see me in a month—sooner if you have any problems. I'd like to keep a close eye on things but I'm quite sure this time will be different."

———

DAWN SAILED STRAIGHT PAST THE TURNOFF TO JILL'S, completely forgetting her promise of calling in for a cuppa, her excitement steadily growing. She couldn't wait to get home to tell John.

She slumped with disappointment as she drove into the garage. The silent yard reminded her that John had gone to the run-off for the day to shift cattle. The dog kennels were empty and the only sign of life appeared to be an occasional squark emanating from the henhouse.

Inside, Dawn unpacked the groceries as the cats wound their way around her legs.

"Okay, you lot. Here you go." She filled the feed bowl and smiled as four furry faces dove into the nibbles. "If you're still hungry after that, I suggest you go outside and catch a mouse."

Unable to contain her rising exhilaration, Dawn hastily packed a sandwich and two bottles of cordial before changing into her farm jeans and shirt. The truck sat idle against the fence and she hauled herself into the cab, turned the key, and pulled out the start button. At the familiar whir of the old diesel engine, she crossed her fingers, breathing out with a whoosh when it coughed into life.

"Come on, old girl. You can do it."

Unable to wipe the smile from her face, she sang at the top of her voice as the vehicle crawled steadily across the farm. Her only stops were to open and close gates.

With no sign of John at the yards, Dawn continued along the track leading toward the western edge of the property. She reached the bottom of the ridge overlooking the Tasman Sea and braked, changed into low gear, and then held her foot steadily on the accelerator as the truck climbed the steep pinch of the track.

She reached the summit and halted, letting the engine idle while she cast her gaze left and right. In the distance, a herd of brown and white cattle moved along the gently undulating fold of the land, one side of the mob pressed against the fence line while a sandy-coloured dog raced back and forth on the other. Following behind, the man on his horse swung wide, urging along a cow that had dropped back to catch up with the rest.

Dawn thumped the kill switch and the engine silenced. Stepping outside, she stood still and listened. John's voice carried in the breeze, his low, calming tone mixing with the occasional bellow of cattle. She waved both arms in the air, hopeful that her position on the horizon would attract his attention. It took a few minutes before he looked up and raised his arm in acknowledgement. Excitement built and her stomach fluttered as she waited, scanning the gully to check if the gates were open. She would stay put until the cattle had moved across the valley floor and onto the fresh paddock before she turned around and backtracked to the yards.

In the meantime, she let the vision in front of her soak into her soul. Occasional patches of sandy soil showed through the grass. Lining the sand dunes and drifting inland in clumps, lupins swayed in the breeze, their shades of pink, purple, lemon, and white painting the most glorious picture she could imagine.

Her thoughts drifted back to her first year on the farm, and she placed both hands over her stomach. They had endured good seasons and bad, disappointment and loss. Through it all, these beautiful flowers had never failed to bring her colour and joy, reminding her of promise and new life both above the soil and beneath it. Now, after nine years, a new life was finally growing within her. This time, she was sure things would be different.

———

"YOU LOOK HAPPY. I THOUGHT YOU WERE GOING TO town for the day?" John dismounted and dropped his reins, letting them fall to the ground. Honey stood still, lowering her head and eyeing them both as if sensing a change in the air.

"I am happy. And, yes, I did go to town, but I didn't stop. I wanted to get home to give you the good news."

"Have you drummed up a few more customers? Do I see this hairdressing business growing?" John chuckled.

"Much more exciting than that." She placed a hand on her stomach and beamed.

John lifted his hat and scratched his head, his eyes wide and questioning. "Are you trying to tell me what I think you are? A baby?"

"Yes. And guess what? It's due around your birthday," she squealed.

He let out a yelp. "AMAZING news! Let's celebrate." He hugged her then and stepped back, holding both her hands. "Are you going to be alright this time? I mean, how can the doctor be sure?"

She shrugged. "He says I'm over three months

already and things are very different this time. He wants to keep a closer eye on me and, I don't know why, but I really believe this pregnancy will be successful." She smiled widely and clapped her hands together.

He wrapped his arms around her again and they stood, locked together while the horse munched grass and a pair of fantails flittered above them.

CHAPTER 27

Hannah Elizabeth Simpson was born on 16 March 1976, weighing seven pounds, ten ounces, and her parents could not have been more overjoyed.

Named after Dawn's grandmother, her arrival occurred one day before her father's fortieth birthday after a difficult birth requiring an emergency caesarean. It was several hours before the nurse placed the baby in her mother's arms and the doctor delivered the news.

"Congratulations. You have a beautiful, healthy baby girl."

Dawn smiled drowsily. "She really is alright?"

The doctor smiled softly and drew a deep breath. "She is perfect, but I'm sorry to have to tell you she will be your only child."

Staring into the clear blue eyes of her daughter, Dawn didn't care. She stroked the soft auburn fuzz on her child's tiny head before looking up. "Don't bother giving me all the details today. I just want to enjoy this little miracle."

"Of course. You get some rest now, and I'll come and talk to you tomorrow." His long, thin face broke into a semblance of a smile. He patted her hand and left the room.

John beamed at her as he perched on the edge of the bed. He brushed a lock of hair from Dawn's face with his finger and she smiled as they gazed at their daughter.

———

A MONTH LATER, JOHN AND DAWN HOVERED ON THE porch of the local hall, greeting each family member as they arrived.

"Happy birthday, John. You certainly won't forget this one, will you?" Charlie shook John's hand and slapped him on the shoulder.

Bev kissed them both, her glossy, straight hair falling in a waterfall over her shoulders. "Now, where's my little girl?"

Dawn grinned at her neighbour. "She's in the kitchen with Alice."

Bev shot her a smile and darted off, leaving Dawn to reminisce for a few moments. She had been to visit every second day since Dawn had arrived home with Hannah, delivering meals and flowers from her garden.

Unlike other visitors, she rarely sat down for more than ten minutes, instead insisting on folding the washing, catching up with the ironing, or running the vacuum cleaner around. Bev was closer to John's age than her own, and Dawn experienced a wave of guilt as she remembered Charlie and Bev's third and final son arriving only weeks after she moved to Fantail Ridge. She had baked a cake and accompanied Alice one afternoon to deliver it, but other than that, had not offered any household help or support.

It hadn't seemed to matter. Bev had always been a busy, social person who, if she wasn't at a meeting of some sort, was driving her children to Helensville to play football or headed down to the calf pens, feeding the multitude of hungry mouths.

Bev wasn't Dawn's only avid helper. Alice and Harry had been more than enthusiastic to assist her around the house, even as she tried to get them to relax. The look on their faces when they'd first met Hannah, however, had truly been one she'd always remember.

"She's the image of Emmie!" Alice had gasped and her lip had quivered as she reached out to hold her granddaughter. Harry had swallowed, his Adam's apple bobbing and his mouth working silently as he stood, captivated.

Dawn's attention was once more drawn to the arriving guests as Harry pulled up with Ed and Hilde.

Still as strong and ageless as ever, Ed carried a large

box while Hilde handed two bottles of elderberry wine to John.

"Happy birthday. These are for you, and this … is for our precious Hannah." She pointed to the box in Ed's arms, and Dawn smiled at the old lady's possessive comment. It seemed that Hannah was not only a gift for her and John, but she was valued by many.

Dawn stood on tiptoe to peer inside the box. A wooden head, beautifully carved with tapered ears that pointed forward and a honey-coloured mane and fore-lock, reached to just below the top of the box. She glanced at Ed with wide eyes. "What is it?"

"It is a rocking horse for Hannah. I carved it from a piece of rimu I have been saving for just such an occa-sion. The mane was donated by John." A grin spread across the old man's face and John chuckled.

"I should have known you were up to something when you asked me for the horsehair. Poor Honey looks like the calves have chewed her tail, and it's the first time in her life she's had her mane cut off."

"Well, it will grow again for her. But for this one, it certainly won't." Ed stepped back to allow Hilde to enter the hall and then followed her inside.

Guests arrived in a rush, most bearing gifts for the baby rather than John. Dawn was a little embarrassed by all the fuss but resigned. They had specifically requested there be no presents, but, in this generous community she had come to love and respect, even she realised their request would have been like water off a duck's back.

They moved inside, and Dawn stared at the spread of meats, salads, and desserts on the trestle tables. *No one will be going home hungry anyway.*

Lillian suddenly appeared at Dawn's shoulder. "Here, you take your daughter and go and sit down. You're not to lift one finger in this kitchen or out there." Lillian pointed toward the adjoining door between the kitchen and the main hall where everyone was milling around, helping themselves to food.

Dawn took Hannah, wrapped in a delicate knitted shawl, and smiled at her mother.

———

LATER THAT NIGHT, DAWN FED HANNAH AND HANDED the drowsy baby to John before wandering to the bathroom for a shower. Wrapped in her dressing gown and with slippers on her feet, she stood by the kitchen window, waiting for the kettle to boil.

The curtains remained open and she threw the window ajar and leaned on the sill, smiling at the bright stars as they twinkled against the inky backdrop. The moon shone brilliantly, illuminating the shadowy line of macrocarpa trees that stood on the horizon and breaking the strong westerly winds that blew across the peninsula.

She let out a slow, contented breath and smiled. It

had been almost ten years since she had arrived on this farm, a twenty-year-old hairdresser with stars in her eyes and expectations of grandeur. She would never forget those first impressions—or how ungrateful she had been to John and his parents. She closed the window again and turned to make their drinks.

In the lounge, John had sprawled across the couch, his mouth open and slack and his arms folded over the sleeping Hannah, snuggled beneath his chin, and covered with the intricate patchwork quilt Lillian had made for her. Lillian leaned against the headrest on the armchair, her gentle snores competing with the television program that no one was watching. Not wanting to wake either of them, Dawn retreated to the kitchen again and sat their drinks on the table. Picking up her mug of cocoa, she strolled quietly through the lounge and onto what had once been their tiny front porch. French doors now opened onto a wide veranda that enhanced the north-facing side of the cottage. A pergola above it allowed light and sunshine to flow through the home during the winter months while wisteria wound around the posts, delighting them all in spring with bunches of mauve-coloured flowers, heavy with perfume.

The air was crisp, a hint of autumn creeping in, and a leaf from the wisteria blew across the floor. She sank into the wicker chair and pulled the crocheted rug from behind her, wrapping it around her shoulders. Her gaze swept over the colourful garden, its shapes and textures shadowy and mysterious. The paddock beyond sloped toward the Kaipara Harbour and its dark body of water rippled under the moonlight. On the other side, beams of light flickered on the mainland.

She sipped her drink, revelling in the flavour. Turning her head, she could see John through the open gap of the curtain, his head resting on a cushion, his eyes closed, and his gentle, handsome face oozing contentment. Hannah's head was turned toward her, her auburn tuft of hair just visible, the shape of her face so like her father's. Dawn's heart squeezed with love for them both.

As the breeze gently kissed her skin, she smiled into the dark. Her dreams may not have been quite the same as they were a decade ago, but she had learned many lessons. Some had been more difficult than others.

For her twenty-fifth birthday, John had given her a pretty porcelain frame with a verse written in romantic script. She kept it on her bedside table and now the words played in her head.

Always remember you are braver than you believe, stronger than you seem, smarter than you think, and loved more than you know.

She believed every word.

ACKNOWLEDGMENTS

I'm sure there is not an author anywhere who hasn't been grateful for the support of family, friends, and professionals during their writing journey. It is not always an easy road, involving hundreds of hours of solitude, doubts, research, and inspiration. However, for many of us, writing is a love—made all the more worthwhile when we receive positive comments and feedback on our work.

While writing 'The Lupin Fields', I consulted many people and am grateful for the ideas, critique and love that you have all shared with me.

In particular, I would like to thank my sisters—my constant support who have always 'got my back'. Loving thanks go to my husband who listens to me reading my books aloud prior to sending them to the editor, providing invaluable feedback and many appreciated suggestions.

Thank you to Lauren at (CREATINGInk) for your ongoing, professional editing skills, and to Patti Roberts (Paradox Book Covers) for your beautiful book covers, promotional graphics and so much more.

To you, dear readers, I hope you enjoy Dawn's story —the second book set on the beautiful South Kaipara Heads farm.

Thank you all for reading.

TULLAGULLA SERIES

The Cedar Tree

The English Oak

The Pepperina Grove

A Tullagulla Christmas

FANTAIL RIDGE SERIES

Peninsula Promises

The Lupin Fields

The Scent of Promise

FEATHERWOOD FALLS SERIES

A Stranger in Featherwood Falls

Secrets in Featherwood Falls

Sparks Fly in Featherwood Falls

Clouds over Featherwood Falls

Coming Home to Featherwood Falls

A Festive Featherwood Falls

THE SCENT OF PROMISE
CHAPTER ONE

Hannah Simpson increased her pace, her stride firm, her footfall soft.

I've done it. Finally! She crossed her fingers behind her back and waited to be admitted to the private office of the human resources department.

This was her chance. After two long years spent waiting in the wings, she was destined to win a position in the hierarchy of well-respected technicians and scientists instead of being the go-for, the jack of all trades but master of none.

Holding her head high and facing the closed door, she rubbed a foot against the back of her trousers, her nerves jangling. The door swung open.

"Please come in." The personnel officer stood back and smiled, her jangly earrings swinging. "Make yourself at home."

"Thanks, Karen." Hannah pulled out the chair opposite the officer's desk and nestled herself comfortably. The women faced each other and Karen sighed. A flash of alarm bit into Hannah and she shuffled forward, perching on the edge of her chair. Had she got this wrong? Was this not the promotion call after all?

Karen cleared her throat. "I'm sorry to have to inform you that you were unsuccessful this time."

Hannah's heart thumped in her chest. She rubbed her sweaty palms on her trousers. Staring at Karen, dumbstruck, she tucked her chin to hide the heat rising on her neck. *I don't believe this.* As shock morphed to frustration and then despair, she found her voice. "Can you tell me where I went wrong? Or why I'm unsuccessful?"

"Of course. You did nothing wrong. In fact, you scored extremely well. However, another of the candidates rated slightly higher and as you know, we must award the position to the highest-scoring applicant." Karen angled her head in obvious sympathy and Hannah blinked hard, her knuckles turning white as she clenched her fingers tightly together. "Do you have any other questions?"

Waiting for a few seconds, Hannah willed her tears to remain behind her eyes and not let her down. Drawing herself up in her chair, she asked, "Was the successful applicant a male?"

Karen stared at her for what seemed like a minute, the vein in her neck pulsing. Then she gave Hannah a silent nod.

Hannah rose to her feet and turned toward the door.

"I'm so sorry." The woman's softly spoken words followed her into the passage, penetrating her head, like a ghost she couldn't shake off. The stairwell door closed behind her with a loud click and she leaned on the handrail and gazed at her quivering hands. She took several deep, slow breaths, then proceeded down two flights of stairs. Pausing again on the landing outside her department, she lowered her shoulders and reefed the door open.

Questioning eyes seemed to bore into her as she slid through the door and calmly made her way to her desk at the far end of the room.

"Well, what's the verdict? Did you get it?" Ellie hissed the words, her face half covered with a hand.

Hannah met her gaze with a solemn stare. Her friend's beautiful Irish complexion had paled, and compassion softened her expression.

Hannah shook her head, her mouth tight. "No, apparently I scored well—but not well enough."

"Oh, I'm so sorry, Hannah." Ellie ducked around the partition and hugged her. "I really thought now that the old dog has gone, they would do their best to use a new broom. Lord knows that department could do with a good sweep—and there's no one more deserving than you."

Hannah pursed her lips. She agreed with Ellie—at least she had believed her hard work and innovative ideas would be welcome. *Apparently not.* "It looks like I'll have to keep on trying, Ellie, like I have for the last couple of years."

"Don't let it get you down. Look at the positives. Now you'll be able to concentrate on the Horse of the Year show and get that steed of yours leaping out of her skin."

Hannah shot her a rueful grin. Although not a horsewoman herself, Ellie loved animals and understood it required dedication and hard work to achieve a good rapport with a successful show jumper. She was right. The new job, had Hannah been successful, would have increased her workload and responsibilities, meaning getting time off to compete in her chosen sport would have been fraught with difficulty.

"How many weeks now?"

"Three." Hannah paused and glanced at the calendar above her desk. "Actually, it's less than that. Mum and Dad are coming down to watch and stay a few days so we can celebrate both Dad's and my birthdays after the competition."

"Fabulous. Let's hope that Hastings weather lives up to its reputation so you can pretend you're holidaying on the Mediterranean."

Hannah forced a brief smile on her face, compressing her disappointment deep inside until she could revisit it in privacy. She pulled her sleeve back and checked her watch. "It's nearly knock-off time. I'm going to leave a few minutes early so I can collect my jacket from Todd's before he gets home."

"Right. Sounds like a plan." Ellie's forehead creased. "I know you were together for four years, but I'm pleased you've seen him for what he really is—a narcissistic bully. You deserve so much better."

Hannah hugged her friend. *You'll never know how many times I ignored those red flags.* "Don't worry about me. I'm not made of porcelain. I'll be fine."

"I hope so." Ellie lowered her head and spoke softly. "You know I didn't believe you when you said it was your horse who gave you that black eye a few months back. It was Todd, wasn't it?"

Hannah shook her head as she grabbed her bag.

"Of course not. I told you it was my horse—and it was my fault, not hers." She leant across her desk and shut down her computer. Giving Ellie a small wave as she hurried out the door, she called back, "See you Monday."